CHEER
USA!

Collect all the **CHEER USA** books!

CHEER USA!

USA!

We've Got Spirit!

By Jeanne Betancourt

AN
APPLE
PAPERBACK

SCHOLASTIC INC.
New York Toronto London Auckland Sydney
Mexico City New Delhi Hong Kong

Thank you to Janine Santamauro Knight and
Doreen Murphy, cheerleading coaches at
St. Joseph by the Sea.

Cover illustration by Karen Hudson

ISBN 0-590-97876-4

Copyright © 1999 by Jeanne Betancourt.
All rights reserved. Published by Scholastic Inc.
SCHOLASTIC, APPLE PAPERBACKS, and associated logos are trademarks
and/or registered trademarks of Scholastic Inc.

12 11 10 9 8 7 6 5 4 3 2 1   9/9 0 1 2 3 4/0

Printed in the U.S.A.   40
First Scholastic printing, March 1999

For Martha Shankman—
a woman with great spirit!

CLAYMORE, FLORIDA.
THE MANOR HOTEL. FRIDAY 7:50 A.M.

Emily Granger glanced at her watch before leaning over to tie her sneakers. Only one more day of school, one more cheer practice, one more night's sleep in Claymore and she would be on a bus heading for the CHEER USA Regionals in Miami. Tomorrow the Claymore Middle School cheerleaders would be competing with middle school cheer squads from all over South Florida.

"I hope we get enough points to go to the Nationals," Emily told the Grangers' bulldog, Bubba IV. Bubba moved his tail but didn't bother to open his eyes.

The door to Emily's room suddenly flung open and Lily, Emily's four-year-old sister, ran in, shouting, "I can go. I can go."

Bubba got up and waddled over to Lily.

"Go where?" asked Emily.

"To Miami with Mommy," answered Lily. She squatted down and flung her arms around Bubba's neck. "Bubba, too."

"Did Mom say?" asked Emily.

"Yup," answered Lily. She ran out of the room as fast as she'd come in.

Bubba followed Lily to the doorway and plopped down again. Emily smiled to herself. Yesterday her mother hadn't been sure if she

1

could go to Miami. The Grangers owned a hotel with a restaurant and café, so Emily's mother was busy, especially on the weekends. But last night she told Emily she would be able to go to Miami after all.

Emily leaned over and patted Bubba. She loved that her bulldog was the school mascot. There had been a Granger bulldog as the CMS mascot ever since her father had been a student there. Her whole family was involved in CMS sports. Her father and brother had been big-deal football and basketball players, and her mother had been co-captain of the cheer squad. So had Emily's older sister, Lynn. Now Lynn was on the Claymore High School cheer squad and they were going to the Regionals, too. The high school's squad had been to the Regionals before. But this was the first year that the middle school cheerleaders were going to the CHEER USA competitions.

Emily looked around her room and saw that the notebook and books that she'd used for last night's homework were still scattered across her desk. She was stuffing them in her backpack when Lynn came in.

"Emily, did you take my silver earrings?" her older sister asked.

Emily glanced over her shoulder at Lynn.

" 'Course not," she said. "You never let me wear them."

"I wonder where they are, then?" Lynn muttered, more to herself than to Emily.

"Mom and Lily are coming to the Regionals," Emily told her excitedly.

"I know," said Lynn. "You nervous?"

"Yeah," admitted Emily.

"Me, too," said Lynn. "It's entirely normal."

Emily was glad that her sister was also nervous, but she knew Lynn couldn't be as nervous about the Regionals as she was. If I were as good a cheerleader as Lynn, I wouldn't be so scared, either, thought Emily. Lynn was so good that Coach Cortes had asked her to be an assistant coach for the last three middle school practices before Regionals.

"I guess I better tell the rest of your squad that it's normal to be jittery," Lynn said.

"I guess," agreed Emily as she zipped closed her backpack.

"Yesterday you were wobbly getting Mae up in the extension," Lynn said. "We'll work on that today."

"Okay," said Emily.

Emily remembered how they'd almost dropped Mae at practice the day before. What if that happens at the Regionals? she thought.

What if it's my fault?

DOLPHIN COURT APARTMENTS 8:00 A.M.

Melody Max stood in front of the mirror and tied a red-and-black beaded choker around her neck. Her best friend, Tina, had given it to her the night before Melody moved to Claymore. One of the worst things about leaving Miami was leaving Tina and her other Miami friends.

Melody remembered how upset she'd been when her parents told her that she and her mother would be moving to Claymore. It had been a summer of upsetting surprises. First the divorce, then moving to Claymore. Her mother explained that she'd been offered a job as editor of the *Claymore News*. "I'd never have an opportunity like this on a big-city paper," she'd said.

"But I'm a big-city girl," Melody had protested to her parents. "I don't want to move. I love Miami."

"Living in a small town won't be as bad as you think," her mother told her.

"You'll make new friends," her father said.

"We'll always be best friends," Tina sobbed when she hugged Melody good-bye.

They'd all been right. Living in Claymore wasn't half bad. In fact, since Melody tried out for cheerleading and made new friends, it had been fun. The kids in Claymore weren't as hip as her friends back home, but they were still cool in their own way. Melody especially liked Emily and her best friend, Alexis. Alexis wasn't a cheerleader, but she wrote a sports column for the school paper, the *Bulldog Edition*, so she went to all the games.

Then there was Joan and her brother, Adam. Joan was an amazing cheerleader, an excellent pianist, and a lot of fun. Adam was in the eighth grade, but he still hung out with Joan and her friends.

Jake Feder, a ninth-grader who was editor of the *Bulldog Edition*, liked to do things with them, too. Melody figured that was because Jake lived in a house right behind The Manor Hotel and was a close friend of Emily.

Melody twisted the choker around so that the knot was at the back of her neck. But Tina's still my best friend, she thought. And I'm going to see her tomorrow. She would also see two of her other Miami friends, Tiffany and Sue, who were going to watch the Regionals and come to the pool party at Melody's father's house after the competition.

Melody's mother appeared in the doorway. She was dressed for work and was carrying a glass of orange juice in one hand and her briefcase in the other. "I have an early meeting," she told Melody. "Be sure you eat some breakfast."

"I will," Melody promised.

"You excited about going to Miami?" her mother asked.

Melody nodded. "I invited some of my Miami friends to the party," she said. "I hope it's okay."

Her mother leaned against the doorway and took a sip of juice. "Didn't your father say you could invite as many people as you wanted?" she asked.

"I mean I hope they'll all get along okay," Melody explained. "You know — my old friends and my new friends."

"They all like you," her mother said. "So they'll probably like one another."

"I guess," said Melody. She hoped her mother was right.

After her mother left, Melody went to the kitchen and flipped on the TV. In a few minutes her father would be doing the weather forecast from Miami. Melody always watched him before she went to school. It was the only way to see him every day, now that she lived on the other side of the state.

Today she had another reason for watching him. She wanted to know what the weather was going to be in Miami tomorrow, for her pool party.

Alexis Lewis brushed her long dark hair and studied her reflection in the mirror. She couldn't decide whether to wear her hair in a ponytail or let it fall loose. Her best friend, Emily, always said her hair looked best down, so Alexis decided to leave it that way. She studied her outfit, a blue-and-black long-sleeved T-shirt and dark jeans. She'd wanted to wear her red shirt with the V-neck, but that was at her mother's. One of the worst things about living one week with her father and the next with her mother was keeping track of her clothes.

Alexis's parents had been divorced for so long that Alexis couldn't even remember what it was like living with both of them. Some kids thought it was interesting to have two bedrooms and two families. But having your stuff in two bedrooms is confusing, thought Alexis, and it doesn't feel like a family when you live with only one parent at a time. More than anything, Alexis wanted to be a member of a big family — like Emily's. Mr. and Mrs. Granger seemed really happy together and Emily had great siblings. Sometimes, when Alexis stayed over with Emily, she'd think how wonderful it would be if she and Emily were sisters and she could be part of the Granger family, too.

But this weekend she wouldn't be having a

sleepover at Emily's or even hanging out with her. Emily, Melody, and Joan were all going to Miami for the Regionals and staying overnight at Melody's father's house. I'd love to go to the Regionals, too, thought Alexis. It would be so much fun, and it would help me with my article for the school paper. Even though she wasn't going, Alexis planned on writing about the event. She'd interview the squad when they got back and there would be a videotape she could watch. But that's not the same as being there, Alexis thought. A good sportswriter is always on the scene.

Alexis wondered what Jake would be doing all weekend. Would she at least get to see *him*? Maybe I'll drop by the Bulldog Café on Saturday, she thought. Maybe he'll be working at his busboy job.

No, she decided, I can't go there if Emily's not around.

DELHAVEN DRIVE 8:10 A.M.

Joan Russo-Chazen had been ready for school for an hour and was packing her suitcase for the big weekend in Miami. She'd already packed jeans, a pair of shorts, some T-shirts, a pair of pajamas, a dress, and her bathing suit. Joan couldn't believe her good luck. She really was going to Miami and the

CHEER USA Regionals. Her strict parents were allowing her to go to Miami with Melody for the weekend. Of course, they had no idea that she was going to be in a cheerleading competition while she was there. They thought she was just going to spend the weekend at Melody's dad's place. Well, at least that part is true, she reminded herself.

Her brother, Adam, had advised her to come clean and tell their parents about the competition.

"I can't," she protested. "They'll ask me lots of questions. They might find out that cheering involves gymnastics and that I'm a flyer. They'd never let me go."

"The longer you wait to tell them, the worse it's going to be," Adam said. "They're bound to find out, sooner or later."

"But at least not before the Regionals," Joan countered.

Adam was right. Someday her parents would find out and she'd have to quit cheering.

It's so unfair, Joan thought as she closed her suitcase. I do everything else my parents want. I get good grades and practice the piano. I love playing the piano. But I love cheering, too — especially the tumbling part. Why did she have to have parents who didn't approve of something that she loved so much?

"Joanie, come eat your breakfast!" her father called from downstairs.

"I'm coming!" Joan yelled back.

Going down the stairs, she heard the phone ring. What if it was one of the other cheerleaders who didn't know about the problem with her parents? What if they said something to her mother or father about the Regionals? She ran the rest of the way to the kitchen but slowed down when she saw that Adam had answered the phone. Her father was reading the newspaper and eating toast, and her mother was looking over notes for classes she taught in Russian and German at the university in Fort Myers. As Joan poured herself a glass of milk she listened carefully to what Adam was saying on the phone. "Yeah," he told the caller. "We'll talk about it at school, okay? See you then."

Adam hung up the phone and took his place at the table.

"Who was that?" his father asked.

"A kid from school," Adam answered.

"A *kid*," said his father. "Is he a baby goat?"

"A guy, I mean, a *boy* from school," answered Adam.

His mother looked up from her papers and asked, "What did he want?"

Adam shot Joan a nervous glance before answering. "He was calling about some history homework," he said. "I told him I'd see him at school."

"Is he a good student?" asked his mother.

"A very good student," Adam answered. "We talk about history homework a lot. It's interesting."

Joan knew from the look Adam had given her and from the way he had talked on the phone that he was lying. Whoever had called him hadn't asked about homework at all. Adam just lied to Mother and Father, thought Joan. But why?

"The word *kid* is slang for a young person," Mr. Chazen told Adam. "Try to avoid the use of slang. Respect language."

Adam, who was eating a spoonful of cereal, mumbled an okay.

"Don't speak with your mouth full," his mother and father said in unison.

And don't watch TV, thought Joan. *Don't listen to popular music. Don't wear hip clothes. Don't do gymnastics or any sport that might be even a little dangerous. And never, ever lie.* The never-lying thing was a Russo-Chazen household rule that Joan used to respect. She never used to lie. Not until she wanted to be a cheerleader.

But why was Adam lying?

MAIN STREET 8:20 A.M.

Alexis was waiting for Emily in front of the Squeeze juice bar when she saw Jake riding toward her on his bike. He waved and slowed down as he got closer. He is so cute, Alexis thought. She felt her face redden. She hated that she blushed so easily.

"Hi," he said, stopping beside her. "How'd you like to go to the Regionals?"

"I'd love to," answered Alexis. "But I don't have a ride."

"Now you do," Jake told her. "My grandmother's going. She wants to see the high school squad perform — and the CMS cheerleaders, especially Emily."

"Great!" exclaimed Alexis. "That'd be so great."

A three-hour ride to Miami — and then sitting with Jake at the competitions! She knew she was blushing for sure now.

"Being there will help you with your article," Jake said.

"I know," agreed Alexis.

"But let's not tell Emily," Jake suggested, "so we can surprise her."

"Okay," agreed Alexis. Over Jake's shoulder she saw Emily walking quickly toward them. "Here she comes," she warned.

"I've got to find Adam," Jake said, hopping on

his bike. "I invited him, too. But he didn't say if he'd come or not. I guess he had to ask his parents."

Watching Jake ride away, Emily wondered what he'd stopped to talk to Alexis about. She figured since Jake was editor of the *Bulldog Edition* and Alexis wrote a sports column, it probably had something to do with the school paper.

Jake Feder was Emily's oldest friend. She'd met him when he moved in with his grandparents in the house behind The Manor Hotel, when he was five and she was three. Emily was too young then to understand about the tragedy — that Jake's parents and his three-year-old sister, Anna, had just died in a fire. "You sort of took Anna's place for him," Jake's grandmother once told Emily. "It was a lovely thing for all of us that you two became friends."

And we always *will* be, thought Emily.

When she reached Alexis she said, "Your hair looks great today."

"Thanks," said Alexis.

"We'd better hurry or we'll be late," Emily warned.

"You must be excited about the Regionals tomorrow," Alexis said as she fell in step with Emily.

"I'm really nervous," admitted Emily. "I'm so afraid I'll drop Mae or something."

"You'll be fine," Alexis assured her. "You're getting so good at cheering."

"I wish you were going to be there," said Emily.

Alexis tried not to smile. That might give away the secret. She pulled a sad face and used a forlorn tone when she told Emily, "Me, too."

CLAYMORE MIDDLE SCHOOL
COURTYARD 8:25 A.M.

Sally Johnson, co-captain of the CMS cheer squad, stood in the center of a group of her cheerleaders. They were looking to her for leadership. The closer they got to the day of the Regionals the more nervous everyone was. When Coach Cortes took over last year, she told the girls she intended to create a squad that could place at the Regionals in Miami and go to the top CHEER USA competition in the country — the Nationals at Madison Square Garden in New York City. Sally knew that the CMS squad this year was better than last year's squad. There were some terrific new cheerleaders, especially Joan Russo-Chazen, who was a super flyer. Sally knew that her squad was good. But were they good *enough*?

Sally looked around at the other anxious

cheerleaders. She suddenly realized that she wasn't that nervous about how *she* would do. She was mostly concerned that everyone else would be so nervous they'd make mistakes. But she couldn't let them know that, either. She had to keep their confidence up. "We're going all the way to the Nationals," she told the girls around her.

Sally's the best, thought Emily. She's just like my sister Lynn was when *she* was in middle school. Co-captain, the best cheerleader on the squad, the most popular, and the prettiest girl at CMS.

Just then Darryl Budd walked by the circle of cheerleaders. Darryl was the star of both the football and basketball teams, the coolest guy in the school, and Sally's boyfriend.

"Hey, Sal," he said to Sally as he passed by.

She flashed him a smile and called, "See you inside." She looked around at her cheerleaders again. Like everyone else on the squad, she desperately wanted to make enough points at the Regionals to go to the Nationals. But she had another reason for wanting to score high. She wanted her squad to do better than the Santa Rosa cheer squad. The Santa Rosa Cougars and the Claymore Bulldogs had been sports rivals for as long as anyone could remember — in football, basketball, and soccer. Now it was the cheerleaders' chance to show that Claymore was best. If the Santa Rosa cheerleaders came in fourth, Sally wanted Claymore to come in at least third; if the Cougar cheer squad came in second, she wanted the Bulldog squad to come in first. Best of all would be if her squad went to the Nationals in New York City and the Santa Rosa squad didn't place at all.

But we can only beat the Santa Rosa squad if my squad is in top form, thought Sally. We can't afford a single mistake. She looked right at Emily and said, "You and your bases have to be really careful when you put Mae up in the extension. Get her right up in one motion."

"I know," Emily said. "Lynn's going to work with us on it today."

"Great," said Sally. "Lynn's great."

Lynn is and I'm not, thought Emily.

Melody ran up to the group. "What's up?" she asked breathlessly.

"Just talking about the routine," Jessica told her.

"If we place at the Regionals," Maria said to Melody, "your party will be, like, this huge celebration."

"We *will* place," Sally assured all of them. She flashed her cheerleaders one last smile. "See you at practice."

As Sally walked away she could hear Melody

16

telling everyone that a few of her Miami friends would be at the party, too, and that there'd be all this great Tex-Mex food, like burritos and gua-camole.

I never thought I'd be going to the party of a seventh-grader, when I'm in the ninth grade, Sally mused. It was like going backward. She hoped that Darryl and his buddy Randy would find a ride to Miami. If they came she'd make sure to get them invited to Melody's. Darryl and Randy were the best guys to have at a party. If they were there, the crowd wouldn't be so young. And the evening might even be interesting.

CMS ROOM 210 8:30 A.M.

Joan Russo-Chazen was mentally reviewing the moves for the dance portion of the cheer routine during homeroom announcements. She didn't care when the chess club and band were meeting. All she could think about was the CHEER USA Regionals. Her thoughts were interrupted by the principal's last words. "And good luck to our cheerleaders in Miami this weekend," he said. "You've been doing a splendid job for our teams at their games. Now you'll be competing in your own sport, and we want you to know we're a hundred percent behind you. By the way, someone just handed me the

17

new issue of the *Claymore News* and the cheer squad is on the front page. What a fabulous photo! They caught your flyer midair. Again, congratulations and good luck."

Several kids turned and smiled at Joan and Kelly, who were the only cheerleaders in homeroom 210. Joan smiled back, but her heart was pounding. Who was the flyer in the newspaper photo? Lots of people took pictures of the cheerleaders when they performed at games. Some girls' parents even made videotapes. But Joan never thought that a reporter might take a picture and that it would be in the *Claymore News*. Her parents read that paper!

As soon as the bell rang signaling the end of homeroom, Joan sprang out of her seat. She had to see that photo. Kelly ran to catch up to Joan as she dashed from the room. "I hope you're the flyer in the picture," Kelly said.

"It's probably Sally," said Joan. Please let it be Sally or Mae, she prayed. Anyone but me.

"Maybe someone in the lobby will have the paper," Kelly said.

Melody came from the other direction. She exchanged a sympathetic glance with Joan. Melody was the only one of Joan's friends who knew that she'd been lying to her parents about cheering.

"Is it me in the picture?" Joan quickly whispered to Melody. "Did your mom say?"

"She didn't tell me anything about it," Melody whispered back. "I guess she wanted to surprise us."

"Do you think she'd pick out one with me flying?" asked Joan. "I mean, because she knows me."

"That's what I'm afraid of," Melody said.

Two ninth-graders passed them. Joan overheard one say to the other, "It should have been Sally's picture. Or Mae's. Not a seventh-grader's."

Joan stopped in her tracks. She was the only seventh-grade flyer. The photo must be of her. Now her brother was walking toward her. She could tell by his expression that it was true.

"Show it to Joan," someone else was saying.

An instant later Joan was staring at herself in a big front-page photo in the *Claymore News*. She was suspended midair in the toe touch basket toss.

People were congratulating her. But Joan had only one thought: How could she keep her parents from seeing the photo?

CMS SMALL GYM 4:45 P.M.

"Okay, everyone," Coach Cortes called out. "Positions for the final run-through."

The music began and Joan moved into position for the basket toss. But at the moment she hit the high point of the toss she remembered that photo. The next thing she knew she was slipping through her bases' hands and hitting the floor on her backside. She saw her bases' surprised expressions as she righted herself and moved into the next part of the routine.

What if this happens tomorrow? she thought in a panic. What if I'm not even *there* tomorrow? The music suddenly stopped.

Everyone froze, as if they were playing Statues.

"Okay, everybody," Coach said. "Normally, I'd let you keep going after a mistake like that. It's what you'd have to do tomorrow. But this is our last practice and we need to end with a clean run-through. And Joan, please keep your cool. You looked too flustered after you fell. We'll do your toss separately before we go through the entire routine again."

"Sorry," Joan said. "It was my fault." She noticed that a couple of her bases were nodding in agreement. "It happens to everybody, Joan," Lynn said. "The important thing is to make the correction."

After they worked on the basket toss, they did the routine again — from the top. This time everyone stayed focused and the run-through was perfect. Coach Cortes and Lynn applauded, and the cheerleaders smiled at one another as they ran off the floor.

"Yes!" said Maria.

"That was perfect, girls," Coach told them. "It's what I want to see at the Regionals tomorrow. Perform like that and the judges won't find reasons for taking off points. Now, all of you, come over here and listen up. Lynn is going to tell you what it's like at the Regionals — from her own experience. Then you can ask us both any last-minute questions you may have."

When all of the girls were seated in the bleachers, Lynn stood in front of them. "The first thing to expect," she began, "is to be nervous. But you should try to act calm. That way, you can help keep one another from getting more nervous. And be friendly with cheerleaders on the other squads. Don't think of it as competing against them. You're competing with yourselves — "

"— for your top score," Coach continued. "The score that will get you to the Nationals."

Lynn and Coach have got it all wrong, thought Sally. We *should* be cheering to beat the other squads, especially the Santa Rosa cheerleaders. Our basketball and football teams are always trying to beat other teams. It should be the same with cheer squads. Especially when it comes to Santa Rosa.

"Any questions?" Lynn asked.

Melody raised her hand. "Actually, it's not a question," she said. "I just want to remind everyone to bring their bathing suits. For the pool party at my dad's."

Sally looked over at Melody and thought, What a show-off. She's sitting there so proud about her house and pool in Miami. Melody better stay focused tomorrow or she'll mess up at the competition.

CMS COURTYARD 5:00 P.M.

Adam was waiting for Melody and Joan when they came out from practice. "How'd it go?" he asked.

"Okay," Melody answered. "But everyone has the jitters."

"Especially me," said Joan. "What if I can't go?"

"If I'd known my mother was running a picture of the squad," Melody explained, "I'd have made sure it wasn't one of you flying, Joan. She probably thought you'd be thrilled."

"It's not your fault," said Joan.

"Maybe you can keep your parents from seeing it," suggested Melody.

"My father always buys the paper," Joan said. "And my picture is on the front page. He's bound to see it. Then he'll make me —"

"It's on the front page of the *second* section," Melody pointed out.

"Father won't be home until dinnertime," Adam added with a little hope. "He had a meeting in Fort Myers this afternoon. Maybe he won't read the paper until tomorrow. You'll already be in Miami by then."

"They'd probably send the police after me," said Joan glumly. She looked at her watch. "I have to be home to practice piano. I'll be there when he comes in. If he has the paper, I'll hide it or something. Adam, you have to help me."

"I hate this," Adam mumbled.

Joan glared at him. She wanted to yell, "I hate it, too. Don't you know that?" But she didn't want to fight with Adam in front of Melody. Melody already knew enough about her family problems. It was all so embarrassing.

"I'll see you later," Joan said, and started running toward Main Street.

"Shouldn't we go after her?" asked Melody.

"Not when she's mad," said Adam.

"It must be awful for you, too," said Melody. "I mean, that your parents are so strict."

"Yeah," admitted Adam. "Sometimes it is. But this cheerleading thing Joan's going through is the worst."

"We need her at the Regionals tomorrow," Melody told him. "I mean, if we're missing a

23

flyer, the whole routine will be wrecked. We might as well not even bother going if Joan can't be in it."

"I didn't think of that," said Adam.

"I bet Joan has," observed Melody.

Adam started walking a little faster. "I'll try to help," he said. "But I hate all this lying."

Melody liked that Adam cared enough about his sister to help her. But she also liked that he didn't want to lie to his parents. There was a lot about Adam Russo-Chazen that she liked. And about Joan, too.

She just wished that she could help them more.

THE MANOR HOTEL.
BULLDOG CAFÉ 5:30 P.M.

Alexis and Emily were on the café deck having smoothies. Alexis raised her glass. "Let's clink for good luck," she suggested.

Emily touched her glass to Alexis's.

"Good luck at the Regionals tomorrow," said Alexis.

"I just wish you were going to be there," said Emily. "If my mom hadn't offered to bring other mothers you could have gone with her."

"I'll see the videotape," said Alexis. "That'll be cool."

Just then Jake came onto the café deck and walked over to their table.

"You want a smoothie?" Emily asked him. "I'll make it."

"Sure," said Jake. "Thanks."

The second that Emily was gone, Jake moved his chair closer to Alexis and whispered, "Are you at your father's or your mother's this week?"

"My father's," she answered. "I called him already. He said I could go to Miami."

"Great," said Jake. "We'll pick you up at seven-thirty tomorrow morning."

"Is Adam coming?" Alexis asked. "He lives pretty close to me. We can pick him up next." She looked past Jake to be sure Emily wasn't coming back yet.

"He said he can't come," said Jake. "It was really weird. It was like he wanted to come, but he couldn't, and he didn't really give me a reason."

"I thought he'd want to see Joan cheer," said Alexis. "She's this big star."

"Exactly," agreed Jake.

"Their parents are really strict," Alexis commented. "Maybe that's why he can't come." She leaned closer to Jake and whispered, "Shhh. Here she comes."

Emily put a big smoothie in front of Jake. "Surprise!" she said. "I put a mango in it."

"I love mangoes," said Jake. "Thanks."

Alexis sat back and smiled at her two friends.

She couldn't wait until tomorrow when she and Jake would surprise Emily.

DELHAVEN DRIVE 6:10 P.M.

Joan's hour of piano practice was over, but she kept playing. She was going through all the fast, loud pieces she knew. It was the only thing she could do to calm herself down. But her nervous thoughts still chased one another. Did her father stop for groceries on the way home? If he did, did he buy the paper? Of course he would buy the paper, he always did on Friday afternoon. Had he looked at it yet? Had he seen her picture? Was he driving home right now thinking about how she hadn't told them the truth about cheering? Was he remembering how they'd taken her out of gymnastics class because they were afraid she'd injure herself and ruin her chances of being a great pianist? Was he deciding how to punish her for lying?

Adam was in the kitchen making spaghetti sauce and watching for their father to drive up.

Joan was finishing a fast but sad piece by Chopin when Adam shouted from the kitchen, "He's here!"

By the time Joan reached the kitchen, Adam was out the door and heading toward the garage. Joan watched her father and Adam come out of the garage together. Adam carried a grocery bag.

Their father carried his briefcase. The newspaper was probably inside. He was talking animatedly to Adam and smiling. He hasn't seen the paper yet, Joan thought. I'm still safe.

She turned on the faucet to wash her hands so she'd be doing something when her father walked in. Through the window over the sink she saw him take the newspaper out of the grocery bag and stick it in the outside pocket of his briefcase.

When he walked into the kitchen with their father, Adam gave Joan a sympathetic look.

Mr. Chazen sniffed the air. "Adam, you made spaghetti sauce!" he exclaimed. "What a splendid surprise."

Joan put out a hand. "I'll take your briefcase, Father," she said. "Taste Adam's sauce and see if it has enough garlic. I know how much you like garlicky sauce."

"Yes, try it," added Adam. "I could use your culinary expertise."

"*Culinary expertise,*" Mr. Chazen repeated as he looked from his son to his daughter. "You two are acting a little strange — like you're about to request a privilege."

"I'm just so excited you're letting me go to Miami — with Melody," said Joan. "That's great."

"I see," said her father.

As Joan reached out to take the briefcase

from her father, he held it back long enough to remove the newspaper.

"I'll just keep the paper," he said. "But you can put my briefcase in my study, Joanie. Thank you." Then he sat down and looked over the front page of the first section of the *Claymore News*.

"I thought you were going to taste my sauce," Adam said.

"I trust you, Adam," said his father. He didn't even look up from his newspaper.

Joan thought of asking for the second section of the paper, but then her father would see her picture for sure. She had no choice. She'd said she'd put away his briefcase, so she had to leave the room. The instant she was out of the kitchen she ran up the stairs to her father's study, dropped the briefcase on his desk, and ran down the stairs. She slowed when she came back into the kitchen. Adam was trying his old trick of reciting Shakespeare to distract their father, who was still reading the paper and had already moved on to the middle of the first section.

"Father, how was your meeting in Fort Myers?" Joan asked.

Adam stopped his recitation midsentence to add, "Yes. How did it go?"

"It was a productive meeting," their father answered. But he still didn't look up from the paper.

"I didn't think you liked the *Claymore News* that much," said Adam. "I mean, it's not very intellectual."

"It's important to know what's going on in your community," his father said as he turned a page. "As you can see, I go through it pretty quickly."

"You know, Joan is a great cheerleader," said Adam.

His father looked up. "What makes you say that?" he asked. "Something you just remembered from Shakespeare?"

"Ah — not really. It's just — I didn't know if you knew that," Adam said.

"I'm sure she is," Mr. Chazen said. "But then, it doesn't take much to yell and jump up and down, now, does it?"

Joan realized that Adam was trying to prepare their father for the moment that he'd see her in the paper. Maybe letting him know a little more about cheering was her only hope.

"We do cartwheels and stuff, too," she said.

"*Cartwheels and stuff?*" her father repeated. "*Stuff* is an imprecise term. It's slang. What is *stuff* referring to? What *stuff* do you do?"

At that very instant her father turned over the

last page of the first section of the *Claymore News* and looked down at the first page of the second section. His mouth fell open as he stared at a photograph of his daughter flying through the air.

At exactly that moment Joan's mother walked in the door.

DOLPHIN COURT APARTMENTS 6:30 P.M.

Melody put her black Lycra dress on top of the rest of the things in her overnight case and zipped it closed. That was done. Now she'd check her e-mail to see if she had any messages from Miami. She sat at her desk and turned on the computer.

There were three new messages: one from her father, one from Tina, and the last one from Juan Ramirez — a ninth-grader she had a crush on last year. She opened the message from Juan first.

Hey, Melody. So you're finally coming to Miami. Tina told me. Said that you were going to this cheer performance thing at the university. I gotta check that out. Same day — night, that is — I am doing my poetry at this new coffee shop. It's called The Place. Hope you can come. Maybe I'll see you at that cheer thing. Later. Juan.

Melody read the message twice. Juan had written to her once before. She was sure Tina had put him up to it that time. Had she done it again?

Tina and Melody had met Juan at a poetry workshop the summer before. Juan was the star of the workshop, so Melody was thrilled when he'd said he liked *her* poetry. But because he was two years older than she was they really hadn't hung out together. This weekend was going to be different. Juan had invited her to see him perform. He might even come to her party. And he was going to the Regionals. Probably. Maybe.

But does he really want to do all those things? wondered Melody. Or did Tina put him up to it? Boy-crazy Tina was always trying to fix people up. Most of the time it was like a joke. But if Tina was telling Juan that Melody liked him, that wasn't funny.

She opened the message from Tina.

Hey, Max. Can't wait to see you. Sue and Tiffany are coming with me to the cheer thing. I told a bunch of other people about it, too. And guess who's MOST interested. Juan Ramirez! It was his idea to go. Cross my heart. I didn't say you wanted him there — though I'm sure you do. All I said was,

31

wouldn't it be cool to go and see you cheer, and he said, "Yeah. Sure." Then he said we should come see him perform his poetry at this cool new coffee shop that night. And I knew you'd want to do that so I said yes. You can bring those Claymore girls who are staying over at your dad's. Oh, yeah, and since he's coming to the Regionals, I thought you'd want to invite Juan to the party. So I did it for you. And of course he said yes, as long as we went to hear him perform after. And I invited Rick — this cool eighth-grader. Hope it's okay. I almost fainted when he said yes. Love ya. Big T. :-) times a million.

P.S. My aunt says no problem giving you and your two cheer friends a ride back to Claymore on Sunday. She drives right through there because of her job.

Melody wondered for about the thousandth time what her new friends would think of her old friends. And vice versa. Tina, Sue, and Tiffany loved to have a good time and could be in-your-face and loud. Her new friends liked to have a good time, too, but in a quieter way. Plus, Melody thought, if we don't place in the Regionals, the Claymore crowd will be depressed. Will my old friends understand that, or will they think that my new friends are a bunch of duds?

Melody realized she was almost as nervous about her party as she was about the Regionals. She opened up the e-mail from her father.

> Maxi, everything's set for your party. Tina called and said to expect about ten people from your old group. Fine with me. The more the merrier. If you want to have your sleep-over in the pool house, be sure that Emily and Joan bring sleeping bags. Can't wait to see you. Love and kisses, Dad.

Should we sleep in the pool house? wondered Melody as she closed down her e-mail. Tomorrow night — according to her father's morning forecast — was going to be clear and warm. And the pool house, with the doors wide open to catch the ocean breezes, was her favorite place in the world to sleep. Joan and Emily would love it. She'd call them right away and tell them to bring their sleeping bags.

As Melody was picking up the phone to call Joan she remembered Joan's problem with her parents. What had happened when Joan got home? Melody wondered. Had her parents seen her picture in the newspaper? Were they making

Joan quit cheering? Melody stopped dialing and put down the receiver. She'd go to Joan's house instead of calling.

DELHAVEN DRIVE 6:45 P.M.

Joan and Adam sat on living room chairs facing their parents, who sat side by side on the couch. The second section of the *Claymore News* lay faceup on the coffee table.

"You know that we don't approve of gymnastics," Ms. Russo was saying. "Especially for a pianist. Why do you think we pulled you out of that class two years ago?"

Joan hadn't looked her parents in the eye since the moment her father saw her picture in the paper. Now she stared at her lap and mumbled, "They don't call it gymnastics."

"What did you say?" her father asked.

Joan looked up. She'd expected to see anger in her father's eyes, but all she saw was hurt. She said, "In cheering we don't call it *gymnastics*. It's called *tumbling*."

"Tumbling or gymnastics," he said, "it's the same thing. And it's dangerous."

Her mother pointed to the paper. "Whatever it is called, you knew we wouldn't approve, so you didn't tell us."

"She's really good at cheering," Adam said.

"Joanie is good at a lot of things," her father

34

said. "Like playing the piano and speaking French."

"And lying," her mother added sadly.

"I'm sorry," Joan said. "I just wanted so much to do it. I love gymnastics. I mean, tumbling."

"Do you love it more than piano?" asked her father.

"I love them both," she answered. "I can do both and keep up my grades. I've *been* doing it. And cheering really isn't dangerous. I haven't gotten injured. No one on the squad has. I don't ever fall." She suddenly remembered that she had fallen that very afternoon. "I mean, I don't fall and hurt myself. We do the tumbling on mats. It's very safe. And the coach or someone else stands near us just to be sure we're safe. It's called spotting."

Mr. Chazen turned to Adam. "You've been part of this deception, Adam," he said. "Our own children have formed a coalition against us. It's very distressing."

"And you didn't tell us there was a competition for cheering being held in Miami," her mother added angrily. "We thought you were simply going for a weekend with a friend."

"It's all my fault," Joan said. "Adam wanted me to tell you the truth. Right from the beginning. He said —" her voice dropped almost to a whisper "— that I shouldn't lie."

"Joan hated lying, too," Adam added. "She knew she'd have to tell the truth someday. That she couldn't keep getting away with it." He hesitated and then added in a firm voice, "I think you should let her be a cheerleader. Just because it's the sort of thing you don't like doesn't mean she shouldn't do it."

Joan shot him a grateful look. But Adam didn't see it. He was looking straight at his parents as he continued to plead his sister's case. "Joanie *has* to go to the Regionals tomorrow. The squad needs her to do their routine. They don't have any chance of winning without her. She'd be letting everyone down."

"It's true," added Joan.

Their mother stood up. "I've heard quite enough from you two. Go to the kitchen. Your father and I will discuss this matter privately." She looked at her husband. "In his study."

"We'll finish making dinner," said Adam.

Joan followed her brother out of the room. I won't cry, she promised herself. I won't cry.

But two minutes later, when Melody was at the kitchen door, Joan burst into tears.

Melody put an arm around her friend's shoulder. "Did they say you couldn't go?" she asked.

"They're talking about it now," Joan answered. "It's such a big mess."

Melody heard arguing voices coming from upstairs. Joan and Adam exchanged a worried glance.

"They never argue," Adam told Melody. "Ever."

I'm ruining everything, thought Joan. For the cheerleaders and for our family.

"Maybe I should leave," Melody suggested.

"Maybe," agreed Adam.

"I just came to say I'm sorry, Joan," Melody said. "I thought maybe I could talk to your folks or something. I don't know . . . I was so worried about you."

"Thanks," Joan said through her tears. "I'm pretty sure they won't let me go. But let everyone know how sorry I am."

Before Melody opened the door to leave, Joan's father come into the kitchen. His wife was right behind him.

"Melody Max," Mr. Chazen said when he saw Melody.

Since Mr. Chazen was smiling, Melody smiled back.

Joan's mother looked sad and upset, but she didn't look angry. "Hello," she said to Melody. "I don't think we've met."

"Mother," said Adam. "This is our friend Melody Max."

"Also a cheerleader," added Mr. Chazen.

"Melody, this is our mother," Adam said, concluding the introduction.

"The young lady who invited Joan for the weekend in Miami," said Ms. Russo. "Is Joan actually staying at your father's house, or was that a lie, too?"

"It's true," Melody said. "My dad — father — invited us. Actually we're going to sleep in the pool house." She turned to Joan. "You need to bring your sleeping bag. I mean, if you come."

"Is Joan as important to this competition tomorrow as she and Adam claim?" Mr. Chazen asked.

Melody nodded. "Yes," she said. "She's really important. And, Mr. Chazen, it's safe. I mean, we use mats and — "

" — spotters," Mr. Chazen interrupted. "Yes. We've heard."

"Well, Joanie," Mr. Chazen said, turning to his daughter. "Be sure to thank Melody's father for his hospitality . . ." he paused, "when you're in Miami."

"I can go to Miami?!" Joan exclaimed, looking from her father to her mother. "I can cheer in the Regionals?"

They both nodded.

"Thank you. Oh, thank you," Joan said.

"Don't be too hasty in your gratitude," her mother cautioned.

"We're only letting you go tomorrow because you have a responsibility to your group of cheerleaders," added her father.

"We don't think it's fair to punish everyone because of your poor judgment," said her mother. "After this weekend we will reassess the situation."

"Okay," said Joan. Even if I can never cheer again, she thought, at least I can cheer in the Regionals. She wouldn't be letting her squad down tomorrow.

HIGHWAY 95. SCHOOL BUS 7:30 A.M.

Emily put her feet up on the seat in front of her and looked around. Joan sat next to her. Melody and Maria were in the two seats directly across the aisle from them. Everyone had on their regulation warm-up outfit — loose nylon pants and zip-up jackets. Blue and white for the middle school and black and silver for the high school.

Most of the high school squad was sitting toward the back of the bus. A group of them were quietly counting out their routine together.

Lynn came down the aisle and stopped next to Melody. "How're you doing?" she asked.

"Great," said Melody.

39

Lynn nodded in Joan's direction. "You did an excellent correction yesterday, Joan," she said. "I know you'll be perfect today."

"Thanks," said Joan.

When Lynn moved on, Joan turned to Emily. "You're so lucky to have a sister who's a cheerleader," she said.

"I guess," said Emily. She wanted to tell Joan that it wasn't always easy to have a sister who was a big deal in cheering when you were a cheerleader, too. That it wasn't so great to have an older sister who was so perfect. She didn't think Joan would understand, though. But Alexis would understand, thought Emily. She wished her best friend was going to Miami with her.

HIGHWAY 95. MRS. FEDER'S CAR
7:32 A.M.

Jake's grandmother was driving the car and his grandfather was sitting next to her. Alexis was in the backseat between Jake and Adam.

"The cheerleaders are going to be so surprised when we show up at the Regionals," Alexis said. "I can't wait to see the expression on Emily's face."

"Joan has no idea, either," said Adam.

"I thought maybe your parents wouldn't let you come," Jake told Adam.

"Actually, they're glad I could come," said Adam. "They like it when Joan and I do stuff together. They're into the family thing."

Alexis noticed that Mrs. Feder's car was about to overtake a bus on the road ahead of them. "There they are!" Alexis exclaimed. "It's our bus. With the cheerleaders. Up ahead of us."

"Slow down, Grandma," Jake ordered. "Don't pass them. They'll see us."

Mrs. Feder moved into the slow lane while the bus continued on. She smiled in the mirror at her backseat passengers. "Close call," she said.

Mr. Feder looked at his watch. "We're making good time," he said. "How about stopping at the next exit for some breakfast?"

"Eggs and pancakes for me," said Jake.

That's my favorite breakfast, too, thought Alexis.

"I'm going to have a cheese omelet," said Mr. Feder. "With home fries and sausage."

"French toast and bacon for me," put in Adam. "What about you, Alexis?"

She didn't want to sound like she was copying Jake, so she said, "Pancakes."

"I guess you all want to stop, then," said Mrs. Feder. "Am I right?"

"Yes," they said in unison. Then they looked at one another and laughed.

This is so much fun, thought Alexis. Being

with the Feders is as much fun as being with the Grangers.

MIAMI. UNIVERSITY GYM 10:45 A.M.

The first thing Emily noticed about the gym was how big it was. She'd never cheered in such a huge space. The next thing she noticed was how many cheerleaders were there. Everywhere she looked she saw girls in warm-up outfits, many of them still lugging their athletic bags and their uniforms in garment bags, just like the CMS cheerleaders.

Loud music blared from the speakers. But Emily could still hear the cheerleaders chatting nervously to one another and someone shouting for a girl named Linda. Emily stared up at bleachers that reached all the way to the high ceiling. The competitions wouldn't start for over an hour, but people were already filling up the stands.

"How many people are coming to watch?" Emily asked Mae.

Mae looked around at the bleachers encircling the gym. "A lot," she answered. "Thousands, I guess."

"Wow!" exclaimed Joan, looking around the gym. "I didn't know it was going to be so *big*." Joan had been so worried about whether she could even *be* at the Regionals that she hadn't had time to be nervous about *performing* in them. But now that she was finally in Miami, her stomach was tied up in knots. She remembered Emily's sister's advice: Act calm. She hiccuped. Staying calm wasn't easy.

As Coach Cortes walked past her squad she said, "The high school squad is scouting out bleacher space. Follow them. I'm going to the coaches' meeting and to sign you up for a warm-up time. I'll meet you at the bleachers." Over her shoulder she added, "Sally, check the program for our place in the lineup."

Sally looked around and noticed a table with a pile of programs near the door. She detached herself from the group and went over to it.

"I hope we're first," Emily told her friends as they followed the high school cheerleaders. "I want to get it over with."

"But if we go later we can see how everyone else does," Maria said. "That might be better."

"What if they're all better than we are?" put in Kelly. "That'd be so depressing."

"No way," said Melody. But what if we *are* the worst squad? she wondered. That would be so embarrassing in front of my Miami friends.

"Over here," Lynn called. She was standing next to a section of bleachers marked B.

The middle school cheerleaders went over to

her. "Since the high school squad isn't on until the afternoon," she explained, "we'll save your bleacher space while you're in the locker room and warming up."

Sally caught up with her squad at the bleachers.

"When do you go on?" Lynn asked her.

"We're seventh," Sally answered.

"Seventh out of twelve," Lynn said. "That's good. Right about in the middle."

Sally thought, The Santa Rosa cheerleaders go on tenth. She hoped it would be an unlucky number for them.

A few minutes later Coach Cortes came up to them waving a piece of paper. Her cheerleaders and Lynn swarmed around her.

"She has the score sheet," C.J. told Emily.

"Okay," Coach told her squad. "We've gone over score sheets very similar to this one during practices. There's nothing new here. But let's just look at this one briefly."

Sally and Lynn moved closer to Coach so they could read over her shoulder.

"There are four categories that make up the one hundred possible points," began Coach.

"Which no one ever gets," commented Lynn.

"Category one is Communication," Coach said. "This includes voice, eye contact with the

44

crowd and the judges, and facial expression. That's given five points."

"You've got to show them that you love cheering," Lynn reminded the squad.

"The second category is Fundamental Skills," Coach continued. "We're talking forty points for that one. But, as you well know, it includes a lot."

"Our motions," said Maria.

"And the dance," added Melody.

"Those are ten points each," said Lynn.

"And twenty points for Cheerleading Gymnastics," said Coach. "Jumps, tumbling, stunts."

"Category three is worth fifteen points," said Sally. "That's Group Techniques. Ten of the points are for synchronization. Five are for formation and spacing."

"That leaves forty points," said Kelly.

"And those points are given for Overall Effect," Coach said. "Which means difficulty of the routine, crowd appeal, choreography, that sort of thing."

"I'm more nervous than ever," said C.J.

"Me, too," said Maria with a shudder.

Coach looked around at the squad. "You'll all be fine," she said. "By the way, we're fifth on the warm-up, so we'd better get over to the locker room."

As the CMS cheerleaders walked across the

gym floor Melody scanned the stands to see if Tina and her other friends were there yet. When she didn't see them she was relieved. There was so much to do now that they were at the Regionals. She didn't really have time for a proper reunion with her friends. She had to fix her hair, change her shoes, and stretch before the warm-up in the performance space. After the warm-up she'd have to change into her uniform and add sparkles to her hair. Sally's mother would be there to help all of the cheerleaders and to do a final check of each girl's hair and to apply some makeup.

Melody followed Kelly and Joan into the locker room. "Over here," Coach called. "Hang your uniforms on this rack."

"Uh-oh," warned C.J. "Santa Rosa."

Kelly turned around and asked, "Where?"

"Over there," whispered C.J. "At the end of the second row of lockers."

Kelly waved in the direction of a group of Santa Rosa middle school cheerleaders who were stretching out near the rack of uniforms. A tall, dark-haired girl who was hanging up her uniform waved back. "That's my friend Carole," Kelly told Melody and Emily. "We go to camp together every summer. We're best friends, but we decided not to talk today. Not until the Regionals are over. Since we're sort of in competition."

She lowered her voice. "I hope both squads place."

"Me, too," said Emily. "I'm sick of the rivalry thing. Lots of kids at our school have friends in Santa Rosa."

I don't, thought Sally. And I never will. You couldn't pay me enough money to be friends with anyone in Santa Rosa, particularly a Cougar cheerleader.

Melody was stretching out in a split when she noticed that the music in the gym had stopped. Seconds later another song began, with a different sound. It was the kind of music a squad would use for a cheer routine.

Sally stood up from a knee bend. "They're starting the warm-ups," she said. "Let's go."

Coach led her cheerleaders back into the gym. Lynn ran over to meet them. "When it's your turn," Coach directed, "line up to go on the floor for your run-through. Remember, you're not throwing up stunts or cheering full-out. Just marking your time. Pay special attention to your spacing for the dance section." She held up an audiotape. "I'll bring your music to the sound booth."

"Next up, Johnson Middle School," announced a voice on the loudspeaker. "On deck, Claymore Middle School."

"That's us," said Sally.

As Lynn led the CMS squad to the sideline to await their turn, Melody watched cheerleaders in green-and-white warm-up pants and T-shirts marking time for their cheer. It looked pretty funny to see them just walking through their routine. You couldn't tell from the warm-up if they were good.

"When you're out there don't let the big space throw you," Lynn told them. "Your routine shouldn't take up any more space than it usually does. So don't spread out too much."

The next thing Melody knew, she was doing a toned-down version of the dance portion of their cheer. It seemed like only seconds later that their warm-up was finished and they were running single file off the gym floor back to the locker room. Melody heard someone call her name. She looked around but couldn't see where the voice was coming from. Just before she reached the locker room door, a hand landed on her shoulder and a voice behind her said, "Girl, do you seriously call that cheering?"

Melody turned to face Tina. Sue and Tiffany came up beside her.

Tiffany tugged on the sleeve of Melody's warm-up outfit. "Is this parachute thing you're wearing a uniform?" she asked.

"We were just doing a warm-up —" Melody started to say.

"Just kidding," her three friends interrupted in unison.

Melody laughed and the four girls hugged. Melody felt tears come to her eyes. She had missed her old friends so much.

"Where are you sitting?" Melody asked as she pulled away from the group hug.

Tina looked around. "Where are *you* going to be?"

Melody pointed to the bleachers where the CMS cheer squad would soon be waiting their turn to perform.

"We'll find a place near you," said Sue. She winked at Melody before adding, "We'll save a place for Juan."

"And Rick," added Tina. "Wait until you see him, Melody. He is beyond-belief hunky."

"That's what you say about all of your crushes," Melody teased. "But seriously, I gotta go. I have to change and fix my hair and everything. I'm really nervous."

"Don't sweat it," said Sue. "You'll be great."

"We just saw," teased Tiffany. She mimicked a cheerleader marking time by putting her arms in a V-formation and jumping about an inch off the floor. Melody laughed.

But heading for the locker room, Melody wondered if it had been a mistake to invite her old friends to the Regionals. What if they made fun of cheering, and her new friends didn't think it was funny? She was supposed to be focused on the routine, not on how everyone would get along. Maybe she should have kept her two groups of friends separate.

LOCKER ROOM 11:45 A.M.

Emily mentally reviewed the counts for the basket toss as she unzipped her garment bag and took out her uniform. She was so nervous that she could feel her heart beating. She wondered if any of the other cheerleaders felt the same way.

Emily was combing her hair back into a fresh ponytail when Coach announced, "We're going back to the bleachers. Mrs. Johnson will do the last-minute check on hair and makeup there. Take all of your things with you."

The CMS cheerleaders were walking through the gym when Lily ran toward them. She had on the miniature CMS uniform that Emily had worn to games when she was Lily's age. Emily remembered how the "big-girl" cheerleaders had always made a fuss over her, saying how cute she was. Well, cute isn't enough today, thought Emily. I have to be a good cheerleader. I have to execute our routine perfectly.

Lily took Emily's hand and they walked along

together. "Lexi's here!" Lily exclaimed. "It's a surprise!"

Emily looked around. "Where?" she asked Lily.

Lily pointed ahead of them. "There," she said.

Emily saw that Alexis really was there. And Jake. Her best friends had made it to the Regionals! As Emily waved to them she noticed that Adam was there, too.

Emily turned to tell Joan and Melody that Adam was there, but they were already waving to the new arrivals.

A minute later the CMS cheerleaders were talking excitedly with all the people from Claymore who had arrived while they were changing — including Darryl and Randy and a lot of high school students.

Joan couldn't believe her brother was there. "I didn't know you were coming," she told Adam.

"Jake asked me yesterday," Adam explained. "He's the one who called me before school when I said it was about homework. I couldn't tell you because Jake and Alexis wanted to surprise Emily."

"I can't believe you're here," Melody told Adam.

"Hey, Melody!" several voices shouted in unison.

Melody and her friends looked around to see who was calling her.

"Mel-o-dy! Mel-o-dy!" the voices chanted.

Melody finally spotted her Miami friends in the stands. Juan Ramirez and a couple of other guys were with them. They all waved and shouted her name one more time. "MEL-O-DY!"

Melody smiled and waved back.

"Your Miami friends?" asked Adam.

"That's them," Melody said. "And *their* friends."

"And here comes your dad," Emily told Melody.

"He looks even better in person than he does on television," said Maria.

"You saw him?" Melody asked.

"After you told me he was on television," Maria explained.

Melody looked over to see her handsome, wonderful father walking toward her.

She rushed to meet him. They were hugging when the announcer's voice boomed, "Welcome to the CHEER USA Regional Competitions for South Florida."

UNIVERSITY GYM 12:20 P.M.

Four squads had already performed. Emily and the other CMS cheerleaders shouted out the chants for the squads as they performed. Coach

52

had said that it showed good sportsmanship and Emily agreed. She hoped other squads would do the same for CMS when they were on the floor.

"Go, Ravens," Emily shouted with the squad from Fort Lauderdale. She thought that the Raven cheerleaders had done a perfect routine that was energetic and fun.

"But their stunts weren't complicated enough," Lynn told Emily. "Your routine is more difficult. You need that to get enough points for a bid to Nationals."

Our routine might be hard enough, thought Emily. But we'll only make it to the Nationals if we don't make any mistakes. If *I* don't make any mistakes.

As the Fort Lauderdale squad cleared the floor, the announcer said, "Next up, East Naples Middle School. On deck, Claymore Middle School."

The East Naples Middle School cheerleaders' music started and they ran onto the floor. The CMS cheerleaders moved forward to the first position in the lineup. Emily couldn't concentrate on the East Naples routine. All she could think about was that her squad was on next.

Lynn put an arm around Emily's shoulders and whispered, "Don't worry. You'll be great."

"Thanks," Emily said. For the first time that day she was glad that her sister was there.

The crowd was still clapping for East Naples when the announcer said, "Next up, Claymore Middle School. On deck, Saint Agnes."

On the first note of the familiar music for the CMS routine, Emily ran out to her position as a base for the basket toss.

Melody ran onto the floor and did a round off back handspring back tuck before moving into position as a base for Joan's free liberty. They rotated Joan 360 degrees before she came out of her liberty with a full twisting dismount. Melody saw that Mae and Sally had nailed their stunts, too.

Next, the squad built a Big M pyramid. At the end of the stunt they raised their arms and hit a high V as they yelled, **"Bulldogs!"**

As the cheerleaders clapped to signal the beginning of the cheer section of their routine, Alexis shouted to Jake, "They're doing great!"

Jake and Alexis shouted the CMS chant with their cheerleaders.

1, 2, 3, 4 — Let's go, Bulldogs.
Here to cheer and make you yell, we're
C-M-S.
You yell it. C-M-S.
Yeah!
Come on, crowd.
Don't stop now.

Now watch the signs
And say it loud.
Yell, Go, Bulldogs, go!
You yell it.
Go, Bulldogs, go!
Let's go, Bulldogs!
Yeah!

After the chant, the music came back on for the dance portion of the routine.

"Every one of Emily's jumps was perfect!" Jake shouted to Alexis.

"I know," Alexis yelled back. "She was great!"

When the dance and tumbling were completed, the cheerleaders ended the routine with a Christmas tree pyramid.

Alexis was on her feet, shouting, "Yeah!" and clapping. To her right, Melody's Miami friends were punching the air and yelling, "Yes! Melody!"

UNIVERSITY GYM. BLEACHERS 12:35 P.M.

The high school cheerleaders greeted the CMS squad, who were coming off the floor, with hugs and congratulations.

"But I wobbled a little in the pyramid," Mae was saying.

"And I lost a beat in the dance," added C.J.

"It was *great*," Coach told them. "Whether you place or not, you know you did an excellent job."

Joan looked around at her fellow performers. Tears sprang to her eyes. She had cheered at the Regionals and the squad had done well. But was this the last time she would cheer?

"Sit down now and watch the rest of the performances," Coach instructed.

Joan sat between Sally and Melody.

"Santa Rosa is next," Melody told her.

Kelly leaned forward and whispered, "I hope they do all right, but not as well as us."

"Me, too," said Joan.

I hope they fall on their faces, thought Sally.

Sally watched the Cougar cheerleaders preparing for a team stunt and prayed that they wouldn't pull it off. Just then their co-captain, Cassie Jimenez, missed her heel stretch.

"Uh-oh," said Kelly.

Perfect, thought Sally.

Sally kept her fingers crossed as the final three squads performed. If none of them was as good as her squad, the Bulldog cheerleaders had a terrific chance of placing in the top five.

The tenth squad on the floor performed with energy and skill. But Sally thought that their program was too simple. In the next performance up, girls fell out of two stunts. And the last squad was so nervous that two of their cheerleaders went to the wrong position for the dance portion of their routine. Sally figured they weren't even in the running for the top five.

The performances were over. In a few minutes the results would be announced. Cheerleaders all over the gym clustered nervously around their coaches to wait for the results. Soon, thought Sally, the suspense will be over. She reminded herself that even if her squad failed to place, she still had to show a positive attitude. That was her responsibility. Everyone would be looking to her for leadership. Her stomach flipped. They *had* to place.

"And now . . . the results of the South Florida Middle School CHEER USA competition," the announcer said.

The auditorium fell silent.

Emily looked over to where Alexis sat in the stands. Alexis raised both arms and waved. Her fingers were crossed for good luck.

"In fifth place, with eighty-four points, Saint Agnes Middle School," the announcer said. The co-captains of Saint Agnes walked over to the CHEER USA official to accept their trophy. One of them was crying. "They didn't have enough points to go the Nationals," Emily whispered to Joan.

"They only missed by one point," moaned Joan. "I'm glad that wasn't us."

"In fourth place, with eighty-six points, receiving a bid to Nationals . . ." the announcer began — *Please let us be higher than fourth*, Sally prayed — "East Naples Middle School."

The East Naples cheerleaders jumped up and down, hugging each other. As soon as their co-captains had accepted the trophy and the invitation to the Nationals, the announcer said, "In third place, with eighty-nine points, receiving a bid to Nationals, Johnson Middle School."

We didn't win third place, thought Sally. Does that mean we'll be second or first? Sally noticed a worried look pass over Coach Cortes's face and realized that Coach was afraid that if they hadn't placed fourth or third they might not place at all.

A terrifying thought crossed Sally's mind. Were there slipups in her squad's routine that she hadn't seen? Maybe Emily's jumps weren't high and clean enough. And maybe Melody didn't do a round off back handspring back tuck, but only a single back handspring. C.J. didn't always remember to smile during the dance and sometimes lost count. Had she today? There were so many things that could have gone wrong that Sally didn't see.

"In second place. Receiving ninety points and a bid to Nationals — " Sally was holding her breath " — Santa Rosa Middle School."

The Santa Rosa cheerleaders screeched joyfully and hugged as their co-captains walked over to accept the trophy and their invitation to the Nationals. Sally knew what Cassie Jimenez must be thinking. If it hadn't been for her error her squad might have been in first place.

"First place!" C.J. was saying excitedly. "I bet we're in first place."

Other girls on the CMS squad thought the same thing and were moving around one another with nervous excitement.

Some of the Santa Rosa cheerleaders were crying. Those aren't all tears of happiness, thought Sally. She caught some of the Santa Rosa cheerleaders looking in her direction. They think we're going to get first place and they hate it, she thought as she flashed them a confident smile. They didn't smile back.

Sally glanced in Coach's direction. Coach still had that worried look and was now biting her lower lip. Only one thought filled Sally's head. What if they didn't place at all?

"In first place. Receiving ninety-one points and a bid to Nationals," the announcer was saying, "Claymore Middle School!"

"That's us," Emily shouted.

All around Sally her cheerleaders were jumping up and down shouting and hugging and even crying with joy.

"Go," Coach said, giving Sally a small nudge toward the prize table.

We *did* it, thought Sally as she walked ahead of Mae toward the officials of CHEER USA to accept the trophy. We're the first CMS squad to go to the Regionals and we're number one. I'm taking my squad all the way to the Nationals. Sally shook hands with the main official before accepting the trophy. As she walked back to her squad she held the huge trophy aloft for all the world to see.

People started leaving the stands. Within a few seconds, Bulldog fans and the Claymore High School cheer squad were swarming around the CMS cheerleaders, congratulating them. Sally was breaking away from Darryl's hug when Cassie Jimenez came up to her.

"Congratulations, Sally," Cassie said with a big smile. "You guys did great."

"Thanks," said Sally. "You, too."

"I'm glad both squads get to go to the Nationals," said Cassie.

"I know what you mean," said Sally.

Sally gave Cassie her warmest, most fake smile. But she was thinking, The only reason I'm glad you're going to Nationals is to have the satisfaction of beating you again.

Emily surveyed the gym. She saw that the other winning squads were as excited as she was. She also noticed that many cheerleaders from squads who hadn't placed were sobbing. She felt bad for them.

"Emily, you were so great!" someone behind her exclaimed. Emily turned around to face Alexis. The two best friends hugged.

"We won!" Emily said. "We're going to the Nationals."

"I know," said Alexis, laughing.

Emily thought, This is super. My dream has come true. We came in number one at the Regionals. She couldn't stop smiling. She hugged Alexis again and shouted, "I'm so glad you're here!"

Melody didn't know who to hug next. Elvia and Maria, who stood on either side of her? Her father, who was making his way toward her through the crowd? Or Tina, who'd just come up to her?

Melody threw one arm around Maria's shoulders and the other around Elvia's and leaned toward Tina to shout, "Tina, this is Elvia and Maria. Elvia and Maria, Tina."

"Hey," said Tina. "You guys were all great. I knew you'd be number one. You were jumping pretty high there, Max."

As Melody was hugging Tina she noticed that two women had stopped her father. Looking in Melody's direction, he shrugged his shoulders as if to say, "What can I do?" Melody smiled to herself. She'd forgotten what it was like to have a dad who was a television celebrity. She ran over to him.

"I watch your weather forecast every day, Mr. Max," a tall, thin woman was telling Melody's father.

"Your coverage of Hurricane Henry was so informative," said the shorter woman who was with her.

Melody's father put a hand on Melody's shoulder. She looked up at him and smiled.

"This is my daughter, Melody Max," her father told the women. "Her squad just came in first place."

"And well deserved it was," said the tall woman. "I loved your routine."

"Such a pretty girl," added the other.

When the women finally left, Melody's father gave her a big hug. "You were terrific, honey," he said. "You looked great out there."

"Thanks, Dad," said Melody.

"I have to go back to the studio for a meeting," he said. "But I'll be at the house to set things up before you and your friends come."

"Everybody's all excited about the party," she told him. "Now it'll be a celebration for being in first place."

"I am very proud of you," he said. He turned

to leave, then added over his shoulder, "See you at home."

Melody was making her way back to the Claymore crowd when someone behind her said, "Good dance. Smooth moves." Even in the noisy gym, Melody recognized Juan's deep, musical voice.

She turned to him and said, "Thanks."

Tina was with him. "We're not going to stick around for the high school thing this afternoon," she told Melody.

Melody hadn't expected Juan to stay for the afternoon Regionals. But she had hoped Tina would hang out with her during the high school competition. She'd imagined sitting with Tina, Joan, and Emily, cheering on the Claymore High School squad. But Tina wasn't staying.

"Let's get something to eat," suggested Tina. "I'm starved."

"How come?" Melody asked.

"I didn't have any breakfast," answered Tina.

"I mean, how come you're not staying?" Melody explained.

"Stuff to do," said Tina. "Meeting some people at the mall. Why don't you come with us? You already did your thing here."

"I should stay with my squad," Melody explained.

"But you're only in Miami for a little while,"

protested Tina. "You can be with those other guys all the time."

Melody wondered if she could miss the afternoon competition. After all, the Claymore High School performance would be videotaped, so she could see it later. And they'd have enough support without her.

"There's a chili wagon out there," said Juan. "I say we *chili* out for the lunch thing."

"Very funny," Tina teased.

"Maybe Emily and—" Melody began to say. But she stopped herself. She didn't want to mix her two sets of friends. Not yet.

Melody spotted Maria and Elvia. She waved to get their attention. "I'm going to lunch," she called to them. "I'll catch you later."

Emily noticed Melody walking away with her Miami friends.

So did Adam. "Where's Melody going?" he asked.

"I guess she wants to be alone with her old friends," Joan answered.

"Is that guy her boyfriend or something?" asked Emily.

"Don't know," said Alexis. "Did she say anything about a boyfriend to you, Joan?"

"No," Adam answered.

Joan hated it when her brother answered for her. She glared at him, but Adam didn't notice.

He was still watching Melody and her Miami friends walking arm in arm toward the exit.

UNIVERSITY LAWN 1:35 P.M.

Alexis and Emily followed Joan, Adam, and Jake across the lawn. They all carried lunches from the barbecue stand.

Kelly, Maria, and some of the other cheerleaders were eating at a large picnic table.

"Let's sit over there," Emily suggested. "Okay?"

Joan had already taken a big bite of her cheeseburger, so she could only nod in agreement. The group at the table made room for them. At first the conversation was about the competition. Then about how terrific it was that Jake, Alexis, and Adam were there.

"Now you can come to Melody's party, too," said Emily.

"If we're invited," said Adam. "I mean, did Melody say she wanted us? Maybe so many of her old friends will be there that — "

"Of course you're invited," Emily assured him.

Jake turned to Adam and Alexis. "I already talked to Melody about it," he said. "She wants us to come. My grandparents will pick us up at her dad's place around eight o'clock so we can head back home."

"Then Melody's taking us to this coffeehouse

where one of her friends is reciting poetry," said Joan.

"Which friend?" asked Adam.

"The guy," said Emily. "The cute one with black hair."

"Oh," said Adam.

"You can have some of my french fries," Alexis told Emily. "If you want."

"Thanks," said Emily. They exchanged a smile. Emily was glad she'd told Alexis she was being careful not to eat too many fattening foods. That's why she hadn't ordered french fries with her veggieburger. But half an order would be perfect. After all, they were celebrating.

Emily still couldn't believe that Alexis came. It seemed too good to be true. She wished Alexis was staying for the sleepover, too.

UNIVERSITY CAMPUS.
SCIENCE BUILDING ROOFTOP 1:40 P.M.

Juan led Rick and the girls up the back stairs of the university science building. "My cousin takes classes here," he told them. "He showed me how to get to the roof. It's got a cool view."

When they stepped out onto the roof, Melody took a deep breath of salt air and looked out at the horizon where the hazy blue of the Atlantic Ocean met a cloudless sky. There were three old iron benches on the roof, all facing east. Melody sat on one of them and removed the lid from her cup of chili. She was surprised that of all the places Juan could sit, he chose to sit beside her. Tina grinned at her. Melody had to stop herself from grinning back. What if Juan saw?

"What are you going to perform tonight?" Melody asked him.

"New stuff," Rick answered for Juan.

Juan turned to Melody and asked, "You been writing much lately?"

"Nothing at all," Melody admitted. "I'm busy with the cheer thing."

"Do any of those Claymore people go to poetry slams?" asked Tina.

"No one that I've met," Melody answered. "It's not that popular there."

"Poor Melody," said Sue. "She's moved to Nowhere Land."

Melody was going to defend Claymore but decided not to. When she was in Claymore she liked it well enough. But now that she was back in Miami, Claymore didn't seem so important.

UNIVERSITY LAWN 1:55 P.M.

Emily was lying on the grass feeling incredibly happy. Some of the cheerleaders had already gone back into the gym, but she and Joan had decided to wait until the last minute to go inside.

67

Alexis and Jake were talking about the article Alexis would write about the competition. Adam was stuffing their used napkins and paper plates into a big plastic bag. Joan was collecting the empty soda cans.

Emily raised her arm and squinted in the sunlight to read her watch. She sat up, saying, "We'd better go back. The high school competition starts in a few minutes."

"I'll find a place to dump this stuff," Adam told her. "Save me a seat."

"I'll go with you, Adam," Joan said as she stood up. But Adam was already walking away. "Save me a seat, too," she called to Emily as she followed her brother. She wanted to talk to him. Alone.

"What'd they say?" Joan asked when she caught up to him.

"Who?" Adam asked.

"Mother and Father," Joan explained. "About my cheering. After I left."

"Not a whole lot," Adam answered. "Mother was looking at the picture in the paper and listing all the horrible things that could happen to you if you fell. Broken arm. Sprained wrist. Mangled fingers. She even had you paralyzed from the neck down and in a wheelchair."

Joan sighed. "What did Father say?"

"He started in on how you're this great pianist and your important career could be ruined because of cheering. That if anything happened it would be their fault because they allowed it. He said they should stop you from being a cheerleader even if you hate them for it."

"I *will* hate them if they make me quit!" Joan cried. "They've made up their minds that cheering is dangerous. But they don't know the first thing about it. It isn't fair."

"Gymnastics isn't exactly the safest sport," Adam muttered to himself.

Joan grabbed his arm and turned him toward her. "You're taking their side again," she said angrily. She thrust the paper bag of cans at him and added, "I'm going to the gym." Turning quickly, she ran away before he could see that she was crying.

IN FRONT OF SCIENCE BUILDING
2:00 P.M.

"So you'll come with us, Max?" Tina said. "I can tell you want to."

"I do," admitted Melody.

"I know the guy at Evolution Records," said Juan. "He's got some new sounds for us to check out."

I haven't been to Evolution Records in so long, thought Melody. And it would be so much fun to go with Juan and my old friends. Especially since Juan knows someone who works there.

"Evolution is my favorite music store," Melody said.

"So come," urged Tina.

Melody thought for a second. All the other CMS cheerleaders would be in the gym to cheer on the high school squad. No one would even miss her. She smiled at Tina and was about to say, "Count me in," when Tiffany asked, "Isn't that one of the girls who cheered with you, Max?"

Melody looked to where Tiffany was pointing. Joan was sitting alone under a tree, her knees to her chest, her head buried in her arms.

Even from halfway across the university lawn, Melody knew that Joan was upset. And she thought she knew why.

"I can't go with you guys," Melody told her friends. "I have to go to the high school competition."

"Why, Max?" Tina asked.

Melody gestured in Joan's direction. Of all her Miami friends, Tina would understand that when a friend needs you, that takes top priority.

Tina looked at Joan and then back at Melody. "You should probably stay here," she said.

"I'll see you at my dad's place at five," Melody told her friends. "Don't be late."

"Right," said Tina. "See you" — she looked at her watch — "in three hours." She gave Melody a quick hug.

"Later," added Sue.

Melody turned and hurried across the lawn toward Joan. When she reached her, she squatted down and called her name softly.

Joan looked up. "I know I'm going to have to quit," she said sadly. "I won't be at Nationals."

"Did your parents already say that?" Melody asked in alarm. "Did you phone them or something?"

Joan shook her head no and told Melody what Adam had told her.

"They really believe you could get hurt," said Melody.

"I know," agreed Joan. "But where is the squad going to find another flyer before Nationals?"

"Your parents let you go this time," Melody said. "Maybe they'll give in again."

"No way," said Joan.

"Listen, Joan," Melody said. "We won. First place! You should be happy today. Worry about the Nationals later."

After a silence, Joan looked up at her. "You think?" she said.

"I think you should be *very* happy today," Melody answered. "You were terrific out there."

"We nailed it," Joan said softly. She looked up at Melody and smiled when she added, "Wasn't it great to have such a big audience? I mean, at first I was scared, but then I loved it."

"Me, too," agreed Melody. She looked at her watch. "Let's hurry so we can watch all of the high school squads perform. We'll see if we agree with the judges."

"Maybe Claymore High will be number one, too?" asked Joan as she stood up.

"That would be so cool," said Melody. "You ready?"

"Let's go," said Joan.

The two friends ran back to the gym.

UNIVERSITY GYM. BLEACHERS 2:10 P.M.

Lily was sitting between Alexis and Emily in the bleachers with the other CMS cheerleaders to watch the high school competition. Joan and Melody sat next to Alexis. As the seventh squad to perform ran off the floor, Emily leaned toward Alexis. "They're the best so far," she said.

"But Claymore High is better," said Alexis. "And we're up next."

Emily noticed that Alexis had her reporter's notebook out and was taking notes on the high school competition.

"Lynn's the best cheerleader in the world," Lily shouted to Alexis and Emily.

"She sure is," said Alexis.

Alexis saw a momentary look of sadness pass over Emily's face. She didn't have time to figure out why because all of her attention was now on Claymore's performance.

Emily agreed with Lily that Lynn was the greatest cheerleader. She looked perfect in an arabesque high above her bases. The whole squad was giving a flawless performance. They had one stunt left. It was their most difficult and it was going perfectly, too, until the dismount. That's when one of the bases — Carmen Torres — fell. She jumped right up and moved on with the routine.

"Uh-oh," said Melody. "That will cost them points."

"But everything else was perfect," said Emily.

As the squad ran off the floor, the middle school cheerleaders and other Claymore fans were on their feet, clapping.

Alexis noticed that Carmen was holding her left wrist with her right hand. Did Carmen injure herself when she fell? Alexis wondered.

"I'm going to find out what happened," she told Emily. She jumped down from the bleachers and ran over to the edge of the small group gathering around Carmen.

"I ruined it," Carmen sobbed to the cheerleaders who surrounded her. "I — I thought we'd nailed it. I was so happy . . ."

"I might have been too heavy on your side for the dismount," said one of the flyers. "Maybe it was my fault."

"No," said Carmen. "I lost count." She looked around at her fellow cheerleaders. "I'm sorry."

Lynn put an arm around Carmen's shoulders. "It could have happened to any of us," she said.

In the background Alexis heard the next squad on the floor chanting, **"R-H-S! Shout it! R-H-S."**

The high school coach made her way through her cheer squad toward Carmen. "You all did great," she said. "You have an excellent chance to place. But we're making too much noise over here. Go watch the rest of the competition and try to calm down."

While the rest of the CHS squad moved back into the bleachers to watch RHS complete their routine, the coach kept Carmen on the floor with her. Lynn stayed, too. Alexis took a few steps toward them so she could hear what was going on.

"Carmen, why are you holding your wrist like that?" Coach asked. "Does it hurt?"

Carmen, her face still streaked with tears, nodded. "I think I broke it or something," she said.

"I'm taking you to the first-aid station," Coach said calmly. "There's a sports doctor there. You just keep holding it like that."

By the time Alexis was back at her place in the stands, word had spread that something was wrong with Carmen's wrist.

Joan leaned over Melody to ask Alexis, "What happened to Carmen? Did she break her hand or something? Can she move it?"

"I don't know," Alexis told her. "I mean, nobody knows. Coach is having the sports doctor look at it now. I think it's her wrist."

Joan tried to imagine what it would be like to have a broken wrist. Could you still move your fingers? she wondered. Would you have to wear a cast?

Maria, who was sitting in front of them, turned around and said, "C.J. said it was Carmen's left wrist and she's right-handed. She'll still be able to write and everything."

But I need two hands to play the piano, thought Joan. And to cheer. She didn't pay much attention to the last four competing high school squads but kept looking to see if Carmen would come back. She didn't.

As the last squad in the lineup finished their routine, Mrs. Granger came over to Emily in the stands. "I'm taking Carmen to the hospital for X rays," she told Emily. "Can you keep Lily with you? I'll meet you later at Melody's."

"Okay," answered Lily.

"Sure, Mom," added Emily. "Tell Carmen I'm sorry she got hurt."

Joan leaned across her friends to get closer to Mrs. Granger, who stood beside the bleachers. "Is Carmen okay?" asked Joan. "Can she move her fingers?"

Mrs. Granger didn't hear her. "I have to go before everyone starts leaving the gym," she told Emily.

"Do you know how to get to Melody's, Mrs. Granger?" Alexis asked.

"I already gave her directions," Melody told Alexis.

The announcer's voice boomed over the loudspeaker. "The winners of the South Florida Regional CHEER USA competitions, High School Level," he began. Joan noticed that Emily, Melody, Alexis, and Lily all had their fingers crossed for good luck. She crossed her fingers, too.

"Fifth place. Receiving eighty-seven points and a bid for Nationals," the announcer continued, "Key West High."

As the Key West co-captains strode out to receive their trophy and an invitation to the Nationals, Emily told Alexis, "Maybe CHS will win fourth place."

But they didn't. Glancing over at the nervous Claymore High School squad, Alexis wondered if they still hoped to place. She was watching them when the announcer said, "Third place. Receiving eighty-nine points and a bid for Nationals, Claymore High School."

The Claymore High School cheerleaders shrieked and jumped up and down excitedly.

"Yes!" Emily shouted.

"They did it!" Melody screamed.

Lynn and the other high school co-captain, Melissa, broke away from a hug with their coach to walk out for their trophy.

Melissa took the trophy and Lynn accepted the invitation to perform in the Nationals. Joan hoped that Carmen heard that her squad had placed before she left the gym for the hospital.

As Emily watched Lynn jumping up and down and hugging her fellow cheerleaders she thought, I really am happy she's happy. I am. I just wish I could be as good at everything as she is.

The high school cheerleaders were surrounded by people congratulating both squads. When the noise finally died down, Emily was standing with Joan, Melody, and Alexis. Lily was sitting on Alexis's shoulders.

"We're going to two parties," Lily announced. "Mom and me and Bubba."

"We'll have our mascot at the party," said Melody.

"How come you're going to two parties, Lily?" asked Joan.

"We're going to Emily's party *and* Lynn's party," Lily answered.

"But you're going to Melody's party first," said Alexis. "With us. Your mom will come there."

"Then I'm going to Lynn's party," said Lily.

"Where's Bubba now?" asked Melody.

Emily explained to her friends that animals weren't allowed in the gym building, so her mother had dropped Bubba off at a friend's house.

"I hope you brought your bathing suit, Lily," Melody told her. "Because one party is on a beach and mine is at a swimming pool."

Lily nodded. "I know," she said. "I'm going swimming two times. Mom said." She looked serious. "But Bubba doesn't know how to swim."

"He doesn't?" said Melody. "I thought all dogs could swim."

"Not bulldogs," Emily explained. "They sink."

Coach blew a whistle. "Okay, everyone," she announced. "It's party time. Go to the parking lot. The bus leaves in five minutes. Middle school cheerleaders will be dropped off at their party first."

Melody looked around to see that all the CMS cheerleaders were there. "Where's Kelly?" she asked Emily.

Emily pointed to where the Santa Rosa

cheerleaders were organizing to leave. "She's saying good-bye to her friend from Santa Rosa," Emily explained.

"Let's go get her," suggested Melody.

The two friends ran over to the Cougar crowd. They congratulated Cassie and the other cheerleaders on placing in the Regionals.

"But you guys deserve to be number one," Cassie told them. "You didn't make any mistakes."

"The neat thing is that both squads are going to Nationals," said Melody.

Kelly joined them and asked, "What's up?"

"Time to go to Melody's," Emily told her.

As the three CMS cheerleaders turned to go back to their own squad, Emily told Cassie and the other Cougar cheerleaders, "See you at Nationals!"

"You'll see us next Friday," Cassie reminded her. "At the Cougar-Bulldog basketball game."

"I forgot," said Emily with a laugh. "See you then."

"I totally forgot, too," Melody told Emily and Kelly. "I've been so excited about the CHEER USA competitions that I forgot we have a game next week."

"I can't wait for that game," said Kelly.

"Me, too," said Melody.

Emily locked arms with Kelly and Melody,

and the three of them ran to catch up with their squad.

12 PALM COURT. MELODY'S BEDROOM 5:00 P.M.

Emily, Joan, Maria, and Kelly were in Melody's room getting ready for the party. The rest of the cheerleaders were changing in other rooms of the house.

Melody wore shorts and a sleeveless red shirt over her bathing suit. Emily had an oversized T-shirt over her bathing suit. Maria put blue minibarrettes in Emily's hair.

Alexis sat cross-legged in the middle of Melody's bed with Lily, watching the cheerleaders get ready.

"Mommy's got my bathing suit," Lily told her. "She's going to bring it and I'm going swimming. Where's your bathing suit, Lexi?"

"I didn't bring anything to wear for the party," Alexis answered. "I didn't even know I was going."

Melody turned to Alexis. "We're about the same size," she said. "I have an extra bathing suit. And I have the perfect dress to wear over it."

"Thanks," said Alexis.

"I still keep stuff here," Melody explained as she opened the door to a half-filled closet. She

80

didn't tell her Claymore friends that she'd left a lot of her stuff in Miami because she'd hoped to move back there when her parents saw how miserable she was in Claymore. As it turned out she wasn't miserable in Claymore, but she still missed Miami. Especially now that she was home. She missed her old friends. And her father. And the pink stucco house that she'd grown up in.

Melody took a purple sundress out of her closet and handed it to Alexis. "Here, try this on while I look for the bathing suit."

Alexis stood in front of the mirror and held the dress up in front of her. She studied her reflection and said, "It looks sort of old."

"I only wore it a couple of times," said Melody.

"I meant *old* like grown-up," explained Alexis, "not *old* like worn-out."

"Try it on," said Kelly.

"It'll look great on you," added Joan.

"And I have an idea for your hair," said Maria.

Alexis blushed, but she loved that her friends were helping her get ready for the party. She tried on the dress and everyone agreed it was perfect, especially after Maria put her hair back in a French braid.

"You look great," said Emily.

Alexis smiled at her. "Thanks," she said. Alexis wondered if Jake would think she looked great, too. Just then Tina came into the room. Sue and Tiffany followed her.

"Party time," said Sue.

Tiffany held out a little bag. "A present," she said. "From us."

As Melody took the bag she looked around and asked, "Does everybody know everybody else?"

"Nobody knows anybody," said Tina. "Except we met some of the other cheerleaders outside. That captain one and someone named T.J."

"Was it the captain with blond hair?" asked Emily.

Tina nodded.

"That's Sally," said Kelly.

"And T.J. is probably C.J.," added Joan. "It's short for Cynthia Jane."

Emily stepped forward. "Hi," she said. "I'm Emily."

Each of the other girls in the room gave their names, too.

When they'd finished the introductions Tina turned to Melody and said, "Open your present."

Melody opened the bag and held up a disc by one of her favorite groups, the Raves. "Just came out," said Tina. "We got it at Evolution Music."

"Thanks," said Melody. "We'll use it for the party."

"You got a poem for tonight?" asked Sue. "Juan said there might be an open mike."

"No way," said Melody. "I haven't written anything since I moved."

"You made up that poem for me," put in Joan. "When you met me at my piano lesson. That was terrific."

"I was just fooling around," Melody explained. "I couldn't perform that in public. It was nowhere good enough."

"It sounded pretty good to me," said Joan.

"Wait until the poetry slam tonight," said Melody.

"So you're all coming to the coffee shop for the poetry slam?" asked Tina.

"Some of us have to go back on the school bus at eight o'clock," said Maria. "With the high school cheerleaders."

"Joan and I are the only ones staying over," explained Emily.

Melody looked out the window. Cheerleaders were gathering around the pool, and Adam and Jake had arrived. Her father was putting out a big ice chest of sodas and juices, and a delivery truck from Best Tex-Mex was pulling in the driveway with the food. It was party time.

A party for my two groups of friends who have absolutely nothing in common, thought

Melody as she turned from the window to go downstairs.

12 PALM COURT. FRONT HALL 5:05 P.M.

Joan and Emily were coming down the stairs when they heard Lily running through the living room, shouting, "Mommy, Mommy, I want my bathing suit."

"My mother's here," said Emily.

"Let's find out about Carmen," shouted Joan as she ran down the stairs ahead of Emily.

Alexis, Lily, Maria, and Kelly were already in the front hall talking to Mrs. Granger when Joan reached her.

"Carmen's going to be fine," Mrs. Granger was saying. "She tore a tendon in her wrist. It hurts now, but they gave her some medication for the pain."

"How long before she can cheer again?" asked Kelly.

"A month or so," answered Mrs. Granger.

"Poor Carmen," said Maria.

"Does she know that her squad placed third?" asked Emily. "That they're going to the Nationals?"

Mrs. Granger smiled at the girls. "We heard it as we were walking out of the gym. It made her feel a lot better."

"Can she move her fingers?" asked Joan.

"Yes," said Mrs. Granger. "But she has to keep her wrist immobile while it heals."

Joan imagined not being able to move her wrist. She'd played the piano almost every day of her life since she was a little girl. Her teacher and parents said she could be a great pianist. But what if she broke or sprained her wrist? Would an injury like that affect her playing for the rest of her life? Were her parents right? Was she risking her piano career by doing gymnastics?

POOLSIDE 6:30 P.M.

Melody looked over the scene around the pool before going into the house for another platter of burritos. Alexis, Jake, Emily, Mae, and Adam were tossing a Frisbee on the back lawn. Randy, Darryl, Sally, and the ninth-grade cheerleaders were laughing and talking around the diving board. But Melody's three Miami friends were hanging back near the cooler, talking only to one another. As far as Melody could tell the only thing her two groups of friends had said to one another were things like, "You cheered great." And "Miami is nice."

Tina ran up to Melody. "Okay," she said. "We figured out who the ninth-grade hunk is that you have a crush on. Darryl. Right?"

"I don't have a crush on him," Melody

protested. "I just know him, and I played tennis with him once."

"Well, you should have a crush on him," said Tina. "He's to die for."

"He's Sally's boyfriend," Melody told her. "So don't go around saying I have a crush on him."

"I knew you did," said Tina gleefully. "And the eighth-grader you like is that Adam guy, right?"

"He's just a *friend*," Melody said. "I hang out with him and his sister, Joan. They live near me. That's all."

"Well, pretend he's more than just a *friend* when Juan comes," suggested Tina. "That way Juan will be jealous. So will Darryl."

Melody saw Sue and Tiffany look in the direction of the big group near the end of the pool. They were cracking up about something that Randy had said. Sue and Tiffany laughed, too. Are they laughing *with* my Claymore friends, wondered Melody, or *at* them?

"The jealousy thing works great," continued Tina. "You'll end up with a boyfriend in Miami and one in Claymore, with that Darryl guy jealous of both of them."

"Tina, stop it," said Melody sharply. "I don't want a boyfriend."

Tina looked hurt. "What's happened to you?" she asked. "You got some weird attitude going on."

"Sorry," said Melody. "I just don't want to do this thing about guys right now. I have to get more burritos."

"I was just fooling around," said Tina, turning away. Melody heard her mumble, "You used to have a sense of humor."

And I used to live in Miami, thought Melody as she went through the sliding doors into the house.

Her father and Mrs. Granger were in the kitchen warming up burritos and putting more chips and salsa into bowls. Coach Cortes was sitting at the table with Lily on her lap. They were putting bean dip and cheese on tortilla chips. Bubba was lying on the floor in the middle of the room.

Melody put the empty platter on the counter near the stove.

"How's it going out there?" her father asked.

"Okay," she answered. "I came in to get more burritos." She glanced at the work going on at the table and added, "And chips. Lily's chips are a big hit."

Melody loved being back in her own house after living in the small apartment in Claymore. Her bedroom in Miami was twice as big as the one in Claymore. All the rooms were bigger, and they had their own pool and a pool house.

"You got a new table," she said to her father.

"You and your mother took the other one to Claymore," her father reminded her. "I had to replace it."

"Sorry," said Melody. "I forgot."

Her father smiled at her. "Don't be sorry," he said. "I had to replace a lot of stuff and your mother had to buy a lot of stuff. That's what divorce is. Things are split down the middle."

That's how I feel about the divorce sometimes, thought Melody, split down the middle.

As Melody laid hot burritos on the platter she thought about how different her life would be if her mother hadn't taken the job in Claymore. I could have stayed in Miami and lived half the time here and half the time with Mom, she thought. Like Alexis does with her parents. But then I wouldn't have all these new friends in Claymore. Or be a cheerleader on the number one middle school squad in South Florida.

Bubba looked up at Melody as she walked around him with the platter of burritos.

Emily met Melody and took the platter from her. "I'll pass these," she said. "It's such a great party."

Melody looked over the party scene before deciding what to do next and thought, Something's missing. What was it? Juan and Rick weren't there yet. But that wasn't what was bothering her. Suddenly she remembered what she'd forgotten. Music. She'd forgotten to put on the CD player. She ran back inside to the living room, threw open the window, and turned the speakers around so that they faced outside. I'll play the new Raves album, she decided.

When the music came on the kids around the pool looked toward the house to see where it was coming from. Melody waved and Darryl gave her a thumbs-up sign. Sally began to dance.

Over by the cooler, Tina, Sue, and Tiffany began to move to the music, too. Now, if I can just get everyone to dance together, thought Melody as she walked toward the kitchen to get another platter of burritos.

When she came back outside she saw the gate to the yard open and five more of her Miami friends come in. They looked around, then walked straight over to Tina, Sue, and Tiffany.

Melody looked toward her Claymore friends, then back to her Miami friends. There were five new people who hadn't had anything to eat, so she headed in their direction. The two guys among the new arrivals — Will and Lee — lit up when they saw the platter of burritos.

Melody smiled at them and said, "Great to see you guys."

"Hey, Max," said Lee. "Tina said you'd have great food."

"Like the party after graduation," added Will as he picked up a burrito.

Melody had loved her sixth-grade graduation party. There were more than fifty kids there and everyone said it was the best party of the year.

Tina told the new arrivals all about the Regionals while they were reaching for burritos. By the time they'd finished that conversation the platter was empty again. She'd have to fill it up for the Claymore crowd. "Be right back," she said.

Emily saw Melody going toward the house again. "Let's help Melody," she shouted to Jake as she threw him back the Frisbee.

"I'll go with you," said Adam.

Melody was walking into the kitchen when Adam and Emily caught up with her. A few minutes later they came out with two platters of burritos and one of chips. "I guess I'll bring this platter over to the people at the cooler," said Melody. "You can — "

"Why don't we just put all this stuff on the table and let them come and get it," suggested Emily. "That way maybe people will mix a little."

Melody smiled gratefully at Emily.

"Good idea," said Adam.

It *was* a good idea, thought Emily as the two groups of kids came toward the fresh supply of food. But it's not a good-enough idea, she concluded, when the two groups stopped at opposite ends of the table and continued to ignore each other.

"Alexis," Emily whispered. "I think Melody's unhappy that the Claymore kids and Miami kids aren't making an effort to get together."

"You think?" said Alexis.

"Let's go talk to Tina," Emily suggested.

Sally noticed Coach Cortes coming out of the house with Melody's father, Mrs. Granger, Lily, and Bubba.

"Here comes Bubba!" exclaimed C.J. "He's so cute."

Cute? thought Sally. How can C.J. think he's cute? He's totally ugly. That dog gives me the creeps.

Looking away from Bubba, Sally saw Coach Cortes smiling at her cheerleaders. Mae waved to her and Coach waved back. Time for some brownie points, thought Sally. She pointed at Coach Cortes and shouted, "Give us a C!"

A few cheerleaders shouted back "C!"

"Give us an O!" Sally continued.

The rest of the cheerleaders joined in on the O and they all turned toward Coach Cortes.

"We're cheering for our coach," Emily explained to Tina before she joined the others in shouting "R."

When they had spelled out C-O-R-T-E-S, Sally, Mae, C.J., and Elvia ran toward their coach and surrounded her. They lifted her up and dropped her — clothes and all — into the pool.

When Coach broke through the surface of the water she shouted, "Where are my captains?"

Sally looked around for an escape route, but she was already surrounded by cheerleaders. It'll ruin my hair, she thought, but I might as well be a good sport. She hadn't finished the thought before she hit the water. She turned herself around underwater and swam a few strokes along the bottom of the pool. When she surfaced she was in the middle of the pool, and Coach and Mae were already swimming toward the edge.

"And here comes Bubba!" shouted Randy.

Sally watched Bubba flying through the air toward her, his short legs beating at the air. As he fell with a huge splash beside Sally, Emily screamed, "He can't swim."

Sally watched in amazement as Bubba sank like a rock.

"Sally, get him," someone shouted.

"She's a lifeguard," Sally heard someone scream as she upended herself in a surface dive.

She swam straight down toward the lump of dog on the bottom of the pool. When she reached him she grabbed hold of his collar and put her arm around his body to pull him toward the surface. She was aware that other people had jumped in the pool, too.

When she emerged from underwater someone was shouting, "Sally's got him."

Sally turned Bubba over on his back and held him around the neck with her arm. He's even uglier wet, she thought as she tried to keep a firm grip on the squirming, frightened dog. What if he needs mouth-to-mouth resuscitation? she thought. Will everyone expect me to do it? The idea was so revolting that she almost lost her grip on him. But she held on. People jumped into the pool to help. "I've got him," Sally said breathlessly.

Emily and Mrs. Granger knelt at the edge of the pool and leaned over to help Sally lift the dog out of the water. "Bubba, oh, Bubba, are you all right?" Emily said as she grabbed hold of her pet.

Lily was beside her, crying, "Is he drowned? Is he drowned?"

Everyone was talking at once. Suddenly, Bubba barked. The partygoers burst into happy shouts and applause. Sally felt hands clamp around her waist from behind. Over her shoulder she saw that it was Darryl. He lifted her up, straight out of the water.

"Give us an S!" Mae shouted.

"S!" everyone repeated.

"Give us an A!"

"A!" the crowd chanted.

Sally decided that it was worth saving Bubba if this was her reward. She kept her toes pointed and smiled at her audience. I not only saved that stupid dog, she thought, but I'm captain of the CMS squad the first year that they placed in the Regionals. That's what they should be cheering me for. As the crowd chanted "Sally! Sally!" she vowed to herself that when she was captain of the high school squad she'd make sure they were number one in the Regionals, too. She wasn't going to settle for third place.

When the cheer was over, Emily hugged Bubba and told him, "Sally saved your life."

"Everybody in the pool for water volleyball," shouted Melody. "I'm choosing teams." And I'm making sure to mix up my two sets of friends, she vowed to herself. She turned to Tina. "You know where the net is," she said. "Can you get it?" ·

In five minutes there were two teams facing off in the pool. Each side was a good mix of Melody's Claymore friends and her Miami friends. Adam stood next to Melody in front of the net. "Where's that Juan guy?" he asked. "I thought he was coming."

"He didn't say for sure," Melody said before punching the ball into play. And I'm glad he's not here, she thought, as Alexis hit the ball back over the net. If Juan were here Tina would embarrass me for sure. I have enough to worry about without that. Melody turned to see Tiffany whack the ball back to the other side. I've put together two evenly matched teams, she thought. It was going to be a good game.

UPSTAIRS BATHROOM 7:30 P.M.

Alexis had been waiting outside the bathroom for at least five minutes. She wondered if she should try the door again. Maybe it wasn't locked. Maybe she just hadn't pushed it hard enough. Or maybe nobody was in there after all. She was about to call out, "Is anybody in there?" when she stopped herself. What if a guy was in the bathroom? It would be so embarrassing. She was about to go back downstairs when she thought she heard crying on the other side of the door. She leaned closer and listened. Someone *was* crying.

Should I tell Melody? Alexis wondered. Then she thought of how embarrassed she'd be if she was upset and everyone made a big deal out of it. I'll just wait and see who it is, she decided — in case the person needs help.

Alexis went into Melody's room, which was across the hall from the bathroom, and left the door open. By facing the mirror over Melody's bureau, she'd be able to see who was coming out of the bathroom. Then, when she saw who it was, she could decide what to do. She was thinking about this plan when the door to the bathroom opened. Alexis looked in the mirror and saw Joan walk out into the hall. At that instant, Joan saw her.

Alexis turned away from the mirror to face Joan. "Are you all right?" she asked.

Joan tried to smile. "Fine," she said. "I'm fine." But her voice cracked.

"I heard you crying," Alexis whispered. "What's wrong?"

Joan was trying to think of a lie to tell Alexis about why she was crying, but she stopped herself. I might as well start telling the truth, she decided. Everyone will know what happened anyway when I have to quit cheering. Joan stepped into Melody's room and closed the door behind her. Loud music from the pool party came in through the open window.

"Was someone mean to you or something?" asked Alexis.

"Sort of," said Joan. "My parents." She leaned against the closed door and she told Alexis the whole story. She started at the beginning, from the first time she lied to her parents about going to debate club meetings when she was really trying out for cheering.

When Joan finished telling her story, Alexis told her that she had trouble with her parents, too. That sometimes she hated living in two different places, especially when she was at her mother's. That her mother was lonely and sad a lot of the time and wanted Alexis to keep her company. "She's always saying how Dad has this great life because he's this successful lawyer and he's got a lot of friends. And that she has a terrible, lonely life. It gets me down when she talks like that."

"So do you like it better at your father's house?" asked Joan.

"Well, yes," said Alexis. "But not always. It's lonely there because Dad does have a lot of friends — like my mom says — so he's not there very much."

"Oh," said Joan. "But your parents let you do all the stuff you want to do, don't they?"

"That part's cool," said Alexis. "Except when I'm at my mother's, she doesn't let me stay over at Emily's so much. You know, because then she'll be alone."

"If my parents make me quit cheering I'll miss the Nationals and everything. It'd be awful."

"It would," agreed Alexis. "But maybe they won't make you quit. You can't be sure. They could change their minds when they see how good you are."

"That will just convince them I shouldn't do it," Joan said. "They'll freak out when they see me doing a basket toss. They don't understand how special it is to love a sport. Neither of them are into that sort of thing. And if they hear that Carmen hurt her wrist, forget it. I'll never cheer again."

"That'd be so awful," said Alexis.

Joan walked over to the window and looked out to see what was going on at the party. "I felt sorry for you when you didn't make the squad," she told Alexis.

"I was pretty upset at first," Alexis said, moving toward the window. "But then it was okay."

"I would have been really unhappy for a long time," said Joan. She noticed that Tiffany, Sue, and Lee were dancing with Randy, Jake, and C.J. Lots of kids were dancing now.

"I didn't like cheering that much," Alexis answered. "I just wanted to do what Emily did. You know, because she's my best friend." Alexis saw Jake's grandparents come into the Maxes' backyard. She hoped they wouldn't want to leave right away. "But it's different for you, Joan," Alexis continued. "You really want to be a cheerleader because you love it. And you're so great at it."

"Thanks," said Joan.

The door flung open and Melody, Emily, and Tina came running into the room. "Jake's grandparents are here," said Melody.

"And they want to leave right away," added Tina.

"I have to go," said Alexis.

"We've got a better idea," said Emily.

"You should stay over," said Melody.

"There's plenty of room in my aunt's car for you to go back tomorrow," said Tina.

"Then you can go to the poetry slam," added Emily.

"And sleep over in the pool house," said Tina. "It's really cool."

"*Cool cool*," explained Melody. "Not *cool cold*. And Tina, Tiffany, and Sue are staying, too."

Emily handed Alexis the phone on Melody's desk. "Call your father," she instructed.

"Please," said Joan. "You have to stay."

Alexis smiled at the girls around her. "I'll stay," she said as she started dialing her father's number.

12 PALM COURT. FRONT LAWN 8:00 P.M.

Everyone from the party was standing on the lawn and sidewalk in front of Melody's house. The cheerleaders were waiting for the school bus. Jake and Adam were waiting for Jake's grandparents.

Emily watched Melody say good-bye to her Miami friends who weren't going to the poetry slam. She imagined how awful she'd feel if her parents suddenly divorced and her mother told her she had to move someplace totally new and different — like Miami. Even if I made new friends, Emily thought, I'd miss my old friends. Especially Alexis.

Alexis came up beside her and whispered, "It must be hard for Melody to have friends in two places."

"That's just what I was thinking," Emily whispered back.

Jake and Adam went over to Melody. "Thanks for the party," said Jake.

"It was fun," added Adam.

"Have fun at that poetry thing tonight," Jake said.

"It's a poetry slam," Melody explained.

"You going to perform some poetry?" asked Adam.

Melody shook her head. "I only performed at this class we took. Not at a coffee shop or anything. Anyway, I'm not writing poetry anymore."

"Tina said you were good at it," Adam said.

Joan, meanwhile, was motioning to her brother that she wanted to talk to him. She led him to the side of the house, where they could talk privately. When they were alone she asked nervously, "What are you going to tell Mother and Father about the Regionals?"

Adam put his hands in his pockets and thought for a second before answering. "That your squad came in first. That you were really good and they should be proud of you."

"What about Carmen's accident?" she asked. "Will you tell them?"

He shook his head no. "But they might ask me if anyone was hurt," he said.

"You don't have to lie for me anymore," Joan told her brother.

Mr. Feder leaned out the car window and called, "Jake, Adam. Come on, boys."

"Gotta go," Adam said as he gave Joan a friendly punch on the arm. "See you tomorrow."

She watched him run back to say good-bye to Melody and thank her father.

Jake wrapped an arm around Emily and gave her a quick hug. He smiled at Alexis before running to the car. Even though he hadn't hugged her, Alexis still felt herself blushing as she stood with Emily watching the Feders drive away.

"Here comes the bus," someone called out.

"Is everybody out here?" shouted Coach Cortes. "Let's have a count-off."

The cheerleaders called out their assigned numbers of one through seventeen. When they'd finished the countdown Melody reminded Coach that she and Joan and Emily were going back the next day.

The bus with the high school cheerleaders pulled up in front of Melody's house. While the middle school cheerleaders filed onto the bus for the ride back to Claymore, Lynn hung out a window to talk to Emily.

"How was your party?" Emily asked her.

"Great," Lynn answered. "We went to this neat barbecue place in South Beach. Very cool. Being a cheerleader in high school is even more fun than in middle school. You'll see."

Emily heard the bus driver call out, "Everybody in their seats. We're taking off."

The doors to the bus closed.

" 'Bye," said Lynn as her friend pulled her back into her seat.

Emily and Alexis watched the bus roll down the street. "Why is everything she does better than anything I do?" mumbled Emily.

Alexis couldn't hear what Emily said over the roar of the bus engine. But she could tell by the expression on Emily's face that she was un-happy about something. "What'd you say?" she asked.

"Everyone's always saying how lucky I am to have Lynn for a sister," Emily answered. "But sometimes it's a drag."

Melody turned and called to Emily and Alexis. "You guys coming? We have to change for the poetry slam. I have a great skirt for you, Alexis."

"We'll be right there," Alexis called back. She turned to Emily, "What do you mean?"

"Everything Lynn does is always the best," Emily explained. "When I went to nursery school, she was a bigger deal because she was in first grade. When I finally got to first grade, she was in fifth grade. I'm a middle school cheer-leader, but she's a high school cheerleader. She's even a flyer and a co-captain, which I'll never be. I might not even make the high school squad."

"You're worried about being a high school cheerleader *now*?" asked Alexis. "You're only in seventh grade. That doesn't make sense."

"It does if you have a big sister who's older than you and is the best in everything," said Emily.

"I never thought of it like that," Alexis said. "But I can see how it could be a drag."

"The worst part is feeling that way when she's so — so nice," Emily said.

"She's not always so nice," Alexis said. "I don't think she was so nice when she said being a high school cheerleader was better than being a middle school cheerleader."

"You don't?" said Emily.

"No. And I don't always like Lynn. She was really bossy when she helped us with cheering this summer."

"You noticed that, too?" asked Emily.

Alexis nodded. "Besides, when Lynn was in middle school her squad didn't even go to the Regionals. Did you think of that?"

Emily smiled at her. "No," she answered. She paused before adding, "But you're always saying you wish you had a big sister like Lynn."

"That's just because I hardly have any family at all," said Alexis. "But you know what I really wish? Most of all?"

"What?" asked Emily.

"I wish you and I were sisters," Alexis answered softly.

"We're better than sisters," Emily told her. "We're best friends."

Alexis smiled at her. "And Lynn is on her way back to Claymore," she said. "But we're in Miami and we're going to a poetry slam. I bet she's never been to a poetry slam."

Emily laughed as she grabbed Alexis's hand,

and the two friends ran across the lawn toward Melody's house.

KENNEDY STREET. THE PLACE 8:30 P.M.

Joan stood next to Sue waiting to get into The Place. There were a dozen or so kids in front of them — including Melody, Tina, and Tiffany. And more people were lining up behind them. Through the big front window, Joan saw that the coffee shop was already crowded with teenagers. She hoped they'd be able to get in. Even from the street the coffee shop looked like a great place. She loved how the whole room was bathed in warm orange light. A percussion band was performing on the small stage. The music, with its intricate rhythms, reached them on the street.

"All of these people are going to be listening to Juan," Joan heard Tina tell Melody. "I'd be so nervous."

"The way you go on about Juan," Melody teased Tina, "I think you're the one with the crush on him."

"Tina has a million crushes," Sue whispered to Joan.

Joan smiled at Sue. She loved that she was in Miami and that she was going to a poetry slam with a bunch of girlfriends. She felt the most grown-up she'd ever felt in her life. Her parents probably had never even heard of a poetry slam.

The line moved forward.

"Next," the man at the door told Joan.

Joan handed him the entrance fee and Melody led the way into the crowded, dark room. It was even more crowded than it looked from the street.

"The art on the wall is the work of middle and high school kids," Sue told Joan.

Joan looked around at big, colorful paintings. Some were street scenes and others were portraits. They were all good and very professional. "Cool," she replied as they followed Melody to one of the few tables that wasn't already taken. Joan squeezed into a chair between Melody and Sue.

As soon as they'd ordered sodas from the waiter, a young woman walked up to the microphone at the center of a small stage in the front of the room. "Hi," she said. "I'm Batsheba, your host tonight. Welcome to another Saturday night at The Place. Lots of talent here tonight, so let's get started with Lyric Smith. Lyric, come on up here."

A girl, who Joan guessed was at least as old as Emily's sister Lynn, came out of the audience and stepped onto the stage. Joan loved how pink and yellow stage lights made a beautiful pattern on and around Lyric.

"She was in our poetry workshop, too," Melody whispered to her Claymore friends.

Lyric looked around at her audience.

If I were Lyric I'd be so nervous, thought Joan. Then she remembered that she'd just done a cheer routine in front of hundreds of people and had played the piano in a lot of recitals.

Someone called out, "Tell it, Lyric!"

A couple of people shouted, "Lyric."

Lyric cleared her throat, but she waited until the room was totally silent before beginning her poem.

TALKING MUSIC

Rhythm and blues?
  Jazz-zzz?
    Rock and Ro-oll?
Or rolling words that are talking rhymes,
Like mine,
  That keep the time,
    And keep you thinking
      As words are s
                  i
                    n
                      k
                        ing
                          Into that special space,

107

That brainy place between your ears.
Let the words in
And find the connect
With respect
To the ideas that came before.

Then find the way
To say
What's on YOUR mind.
In rhyme.
That keeps time.
Line by line
Like mine.
DO IT!

Joan loved how Lyric performed the words of her poem by saying some words louder than others and pausing after some of the lines.

The crowd broke into applause. Someone shouted, "Yes, Lyric."

Lyric smiled, put the mike back on its stand, and left the stage.

While the next poet was taking the stage, Melody spotted Juan with a group of friends at a table toward the front of the room. She wondered if he even knew she was there. Just then he looked back and saw her staring at him.

He waved.

Tina elbowed her.

"I know," Melody told Tina under her breath. "I saw him."

Melody didn't recognize either of the next two performers, but she loved their poetry. She vowed to herself that she would start writing poetry again soon. It would be a lot easier to be a poet if I still lived in Miami, she thought. My friends here are interested in poetry. And I'd come to The Place all the time.

Batsheba was at the mike again. "Next up is a newcomer to The Place's Saturday Night Poetry Slam. Please welcome Juan Ramirez."

"Go, Juan!" shouted Tina.

A few people turned around to check out Juan's big fan. But Melody knew that Tina didn't care. She wasn't shy. Melody thought it wouldn't be long before Tina started performing at poetry slams.

Juan walked onstage carrying a small drum, which he put down on a stool that was in the center of the stage. Melody wondered if he was nervous. He probably is, she thought, but he's so cool he doesn't show it. She remembered how nervous she was at the Regionals. How nervous the whole squad was. They'd acted cool, too.

Juan looked confidently around the audience as he adjusted the mike to his height. Then he began an even beat on the drum. His drum riff became softer as he began his poem.

THE BEAT

Beat
Beat
Beat
I hit the beat,
    The street beat
        That moves my feet
To where I want to be.

Uptown
Downtown
Out of town
Going to hit the road
To see a load
Of new spaces,
    Places I've never been.
When?
Whenever I can
Because I am a moving man
    A fan
        of all the peoples of the world.
Africa,
Latin America,
Australia, Asia, and Iceland, too.
Want to . . . want to . . . want to
Go places,
Hear things,
The ring of the words of many peoples
And feel their beat

The heartbeat that says,
"I am here
   And so are you.
      How do you do?"
Do.
Do.
Do meet
And keep the beat
The heartbeat
Of the world.

After Juan recited the last line, he kept drumming a heartbeat. It was the only sound in the room. Melody felt her own heartbeat keeping pace with the drum.

When Juan stopped there was a second of silence, then the audience applauded loudly. Melody knew that Juan's first appearance at The Place was a big success.

During a break in the poetry performances, Juan came over to Melody and her friends to say hi and thank them for coming.

"You were great," Melody told him.

"You going to do something next Saturday?" asked Tina.

"Hope so," he said.

"I'll be here," Tina told him.

But I won't, thought Melody sadly.

Emily noticed that lots of kids came over

111

to the table to say hi to Melody. No wonder she wasn't happy when she first came to Claymore, thought Emily. She left a lot of friends behind.

VAN 10:30 P.M.

Tina's mother was waiting for Melody and her friends outside The Place. Melody, Tina, and Joan took the backseat. Alexis sat with Emily and Sue in the middle seat. And Tiffany sat up front with Tina's mother.

When the van slowly made its way down a wide, busy street, Alexis studied the passing scene through the window. To her left, she saw a boardwalk along a sandy beach that led to the ocean. Even though it was late at night, people were skateboarding and Rollerblading on the boardwalk. On the other side of the street there were colorful and brightly lit hotels and restaurants as far as she could see. The outdoor restaurants and cafés were crowded with people. Miami was a lot different from quiet Claymore, where there was only one hotel.

Alexis asked Sue, "Do you do stuff like this every weekend?"

"There's always something fun to do in Miami," Sue answered. "But I'm mostly busy with the swim team. Melody was on the swim team, too."

"And now I'm a cheerleader," said Melody.

"Give us an M!" shouted Tina.

"M!" everyone in the van hollered.

"E!" shouted Tina.

"E!" the rest of the girls repeated.

But instead of continuing to spell out Melody's name by shouting L, Tina next shouted, "What does it spell?"

"Me?" the girls asked in unison.

"Louder!" shouted Tina.

"Me!" everyone yelled back to her.

Then they broke out laughing.

Melody noticed that her Claymore friends were laughing just as hard as her Miami friends. They appreciated Tina's offbeat sense of humor, too. Maybe her two sets of friends weren't so different after all.

12 PALM COURT. POOLSIDE 11:30 P.M.

Melody sat at the edge of the pool, her feet dangling in the water. Emily and Sue were talking about the poetry slam and treading water at the deep end. Alexis and Tiffany had just climbed out of the pool and were drying off while they talked about their favorite women pro basketball players. Tina and Joan were arranging the sleeping bags in the pool house and talking about Adam. Tina said that Joan must love having an older brother because then she'd meet all these cool older guys.

"Adam likes to hang out with my friends," Melody heard Joan telling Tina.

Melody smiled to herself. She was glad that Adam liked to hang out with them. She slipped into the water for one last swim before going to bed. After swimming a few strokes she rolled over on her back to float and look at the stars. A poem she'd written last summer came into her mind.

Split.
Separated.
Divorced.
Mom, Dad, and me
Are not a family of three
Like we used to be.
Now it's Mom and me
Or Dad and me.
Only two at a time.
So why this rhyme?
Because I can't see
Why it has to be
That we are no longer three.

Melody had never shared that rhyme with anyone. Reciting the poem to herself reminded her of all the confusion and hurt she'd felt when her parents told her they were divorcing. I hate it, she thought.

"Hey, Melody," Tina called. "Do you want to

sleep on the end or in the middle, between me and Joan?"

"In the middle," Melody called back to her. At least I got my two sets of friends together, she thought. They don't have to be separated all the time like my parents.

As Melody watched Emily and Sue climbing out of the pool she had an idea. She swam over toward the edge of the pool herself and called to them, "Go over to the pool house. I want to take a group picture. Tell the others."

By the time Melody got out of the water, her best friends from Miami and her best friends from Claymore were at the pool house talking and having a great time together while they waited for her. She took her camera out of her backpack and went over to them.

"Okay," she directed, "Joan and Tina up front, since — "

" — since we're the shortest," Joan and Tina said in unison.

"And I'll sit in front of them," suggested Sue, "because I'm the — "

" — ugliest," teased Tiffany.

"I was going to say *tallest*," explained Sue, pretending her feelings had been hurt.

"You're the *prettiest*, Sue," Emily said.

"Thank you, Emily," said Sue, still acting offended. "You have good taste."

Emily, Tiffany, and Alexis stood behind Tina, Joan, and Sue. Tina held up a blue-and-white striped towel like a flag. "CMS colors," she said. "For the day your squad was number one in all of South Florida."

"Yea!" Melody's six friends yelled.

At that instant Melody took a photo of her three friends from one coast of Florida — where her father lived — and three from the other coast — where she and her mother lived. Six friends who knew and liked her and now liked one another.

POOL HOUSE 11:55 P.M.

Emily lay thinking in her sleeping bag. It had been such a special day she didn't want it to end. But no one was talking anymore, and she could tell by the slow breathing coming from Tiffany's sleeping bag that she was asleep. The only other sound was the water gently lapping against the sides of the pool. Emily sat up on her elbows for one last look at the starlit sky before going to sleep.

"'Night, Emily," whispered Alexis in a sleepy voice. "Congratulations. You were great."

"Thanks," Emily whispered back as she slipped down into her sleeping bag. "Good night."

As soon as Emily closed her eyes she felt like

she was at the Regionals again. Running out to take her position. Hoisting Mae up in one smooth motion. Smiling at the crowds and shouting out the chant. She'd loved every minute of it.

Alexis turned over to make herself more comfortable. It had been a fabulous day — from the moment that Jake picked her up early that morning. Now that all the cheering and partying were over, she was thinking about her article for the *Bulldog Edition*. She'd made lots of notes and would be writing a firsthand account — both from her notes and her memories. Claymore Middle School had placed first in the Regionals — that made her column especially important. I'll work on it as soon as I get home tomorrow, she told herself. I'll write about the high school competition, too, but not about Carmen getting injured. I don't want to make a big deal about it in case Joan's parents read my article. That was Alexis's last thought before falling asleep.

Joan wasn't sleeping yet. She was also thinking about Carmen's injury. What if it had happened to me? she wondered. Would I still be able to play the piano? Were her parents right? Was she really risking her career as a pianist by being a cheerleader? But she'd be so unhappy if she couldn't cheer. She'd have to do everything she could to convince her parents to let her stay on the squad. Everything but lie. Joan promised herself that she wasn't going to lie again. Not to her parents. Not to Adam. Not to her friends.

Melody lay awake long after her friends had fallen asleep. The events of the day kept going through her head. She tried counting sheep, but the sheep turned into tumbling cheerleaders. Finally, she slid out of her sleeping bag and went into the house. As she walked through the rooms she was flooded with memories of her life here. In the living room she remembered how her parents played board games with her when she was little. They always had a great time — the three of them together. In the kitchen she remembered how her father had taught her to cook. And how happy her mother was when she came home late from work and found dinner ready. They'd always fooled around and joked together — the three of them. As hard as Melody thought about it, she couldn't remember her parents fighting. Not once.

She climbed the stairs to her old room, went to her desk, and turned on the light. Her friends' clothes and overnight bags were scattered all over the place. She took Tina's black skirt off the back of the desk chair and Emily's bag off the desk. But before sitting down she carried her chair over to the closet door, stood on the chair, and reached up along the top of the molding. Her fingers found the key she'd left there. She used it to open the bottom right-hand drawer of her desk. Inside was a pile of diaries she'd started keeping when she was seven years old. She took out the last diary, but it was only half full. Melody knew the exact day she'd stopped writing in it — the twenty-fourth of June, last summer. The day before her parents told her about the divorce.

I'm going to take this diary to Claymore with me, she thought. That's where I live now, so that's where my diary should be. She stuffed the diary into the bottom of her overnight bag, locked the drawer, put the key back on top of the molding, and left her bedroom.

As Melody walked back down the stairs to the pool house, she thought about what she'd put in her diary. She supposed she'd write about the divorce, but mostly she wanted to write about her new life in Claymore and what it was like to be a cheerleader on the number one squad in South Florida.

Maybe by the time we go to Nationals, she thought, I'll have started a new book.

ABOUT THE AUTHOR

Jeanne Betancourt has written many novels for young adults, several of which have won Children's Choice awards. She also writes the popular Pony Pal series for younger readers.

Jeanne lives in New York City and Sharon, Connecticut, with her husband, two cats, and a dog. Her hobbies include drawing, painting, hiking, swimming, and tap dancing. Like the girls in CHEER USA, she was a cheerleader in middle school.